To Chris...
Andie

Welcome to our family

Happy Thanksgiving.

Jerry & Renee
Catt

11-22-18

MWE1613592

Operation Geronimo

A Novel

James Castellano

Operation Geronimo is a work of fiction. The names, characters, places, and incidents portrayed in the story are a product of the author's imagination or have been used fictitiously. Any resemblance to actual persons, living or dead, businesses, companies, events, or locales, is entirely coincidental.

Operation Geronimo
Copyright © 2015 by James Castellano
All rights reserved
Printed in the United States of America
ISBN: 978-0-9964285-0-7

No part of this book may be used or reproduced in any manner whatsoever without written permission except in the case of brief quotations embodied in critical articles and reviews.

For information, contact
Austin Brothers Publishing
3616 Sutter Ct.
Fort Worth, TX 76137

www.austinbrotherspublishing.com

CONTENTS

FOREWORD

I never felt that writing would become such a passion. However, on Thanksgiving evening, 2007, I decided to try my hand and write a book on leadership. About 50 pages into it I realized the whole thing bored me to tears. How would the reader feel? So I took a different direction, using a story to convey my ideas. That's when the fun began.

I embarked on a rollercoaster ride learning just how tough it can be writing good fiction. Everything I learned in high school, and college English classes no longer applied. I had to learn minor things, such as Point of View, active versus passive writing, and eliminating the dreaded adverbs. Who'd have ever thought about "showing, not telling?" A long journey, spending countless hours reading how-to books, going to conferences, and rewrite after rewrite, to learn this crazy, frustrating, yet rewarding craft.

There are a few people I need to thank. Without them, writing would not have been possible:

Of course, first and foremost is our Savior, Jesus Christ, who makes all things possible.

On the Spiritual side I want to thank these men for helping me understand how to be a *Real Man*: Ronnie Holmes, Church of the Open Door, Bellmead, TX, Randy Landis, LifeChurch, Allentown, PA, James Sohaney, Kingdom Life Family Center, Allentown, PA, Tony Adamo, Kingdom Life Family Center, Allentown, PA

On the writing side of things, it starts with Marlene Bagnull, the founder of the *Greater Philly Christian Writers Conference*, and *The Colorado Christian Writers Conference*. She had the privilege (and I use this term loosely) of editing my first ever fiction draft. She taught me many things, including what a POV is. Thank you Marlene.

When we moved to Tyler in 2012, I had the honor to participate in a writers group headed up by Sandi Tompkins, another great writing teacher, who critiqued my work without mercy, which is now much appreciated. Thank you Sandi T, Sandy D, and the rest of the Tyler group.

My personal coach, Tim Randolph, who helps me in all areas. Tim introduced me to Terry Austin, who published this book. Thank you Tim and Terry.

I also want to thank my mother, my children and grandchildren for their love, support, and encouragement as I made them read my trash, and they told me how good it was.

Most important though is my best friend, my confidant, my mortal pillar of strength, my wife, Rosemary, also known as *Muneca*. She totally understands me, loves me, and lets me go after my dreams. She inspires me to achieve things I'd never dreamed of. Without her in my life, there'd be no reason to achieve these things. Not only do I thank you, *Mi Muneca*, I love you!

James L Castellano

Operation Geronimo

CHAPTER ONE

Monday, August 22, 2010 10:15 AM
Pine Street Office

My cell buzzed. *Restricted* appeared on the screen. Something told me not to answer..

"Green?" an unfamiliar voice spoke.

"Yes," I answered. "Who's calling?"

"Don't worry about who I am. Worry about what I know."

I lifted my feet onto the edge of my desk, forcing the backrest of my chair to recline. I've made plenty of enemies buying and destroying companies over the years. Must be one of those losers who cry foul every time someone gets canned.

"Tell me what you know. . . son."

"Times Square tomorrow at 3:00."

"I'm not going anywhere. Whatever you need to tell me, you can tell me right now."

"No Green. In person."

"I'm not wasting my time with a maggot like you. I got a business to run," I told him and hung up.

I walked to my office window overlooking the New York skyline. Between the super-structures lies a breathtaking view of the Hudson River. Beyond the river, the New Jersey shoreline sports its seasonal beauty.

Autumn brings about a special time in the Northeast. The trees show-off their boldest colors in preparation for the upcoming dormancy. The thick lawns boast a lushness you can almost feel sprouting between your toes. Today's one of those special days. No creep's going to ruin it.

My cell buzzed again.

"What do you want?" I answered.

"You think this is a game?" Same guy, different tone.

"Look, pal. I told you I got no time for punks like you. State your claim or shut your mouth."

"Joe Sperry had a few secrets."

"And?"

"And...you knew about them."

"Yes, they're all public info now."

"All...except one."

I walked back to my desk and sat down. "I don't know what you're talking about."

"You sure? Come on Green, think."

I started to sweat. What's he getting at? "Go play your games somewhere else."

"You and Joe had a secret," he said. "You know what I'm talking about."

I rose from my chair, walking to the window again trying to imagine who this could be. Every investor at my level finds tidbits of information we develop into ammunition to feed our proverbial, smoking gun. My blood pressure started to rise. This may be bad.

"You have nothing pal," I said buying time to think. "You don't know who you're dealing with."

"You're wrong Green. I know exactly who I'm dealing with."

"What if I refuse?"

"You'll leave me no choice."

My hand started to tremble and my voice cracked as I spoke. "No choice for what?"

"Why, I'll get the fed's involved, of course. That should be fun."

The sweat started running down my face. "How will I know you?"

"You won't."

He stayed quiet. I wiped the sweat from my forehead using my shirt sleeve.

"Stand in front of the NASDAQ building facing the street. Don't bring any of your loser friends either. You and you alone."

"I'll be there, but I'm not coming alone."

"Alone or you'll be sorry."

"How do I know you're not some lunatic looking to put a knife in my back?"

"You don't. You'll have to take your chances."

"I'll be there, and so help me God, if you're. . ."

He laughed and hung up. I called Ty.

Ty Gillian is my long time assistant. He came with me from Rogers when I started Green Enterprises. Our ambitions have a similar tone. He wants to be a major player in the world of high-finance. My goal is to be the most feared man on *the street*. I want everyone to know who I am. I'm well on my way.

"Ty, we've got a problem."

"What?"

"Some clown says he knows about Sperry. If I don't meet him tomorrow he goes to the AG. Not good."

"Is he legit?"

"I don't know, but the timing's terrible."

"Why's that?"

"I'm headed over to Stephen's office right now to do another deposition on Sperry. I'm beginning to regret this deal."

"I thought you had it wrapped up?"

"We did until their lawyer convinced the spoiled rotten Sperry kids they could get more than we offered."

"Two million's not enough these days?"

"Guess not," I said. "I'll see you tomorrow." End call.

A sail boat cruising the Hudson caught my attention. From this distance, the boat's size appeared small, but up close its length would measure well over 50 feet—a perfect size to get lost in. Getting lost would do wonders for me right about now.

I shot Rasta a text. *Come pic me up. Have appt midtown.*

Monday, August 22, 2010 11:00 AM
Pine Street Office

My phone buzzed again. With hesitation I peeked at the screen.

Rasta, thank God.

"Hey, boss man got your text? Need me today?"

"Today and tomorrow. When can you be here?"

"I pick you up in 15 minutes. Where we going today, boss man?"

"Midtown to Stephens' office."

"Ahh, yes, your lawyer. I'm on my way."

I make it a point to circle the floor, taking the long way to the VIP elevator. This route takes me past the offices of BQE, *Beauty Queen Especiale*. There's always a pleasant view.

I love this building. All floors above the 45th have access to the express VIP elevators. It takes less than 10 seconds to get up or down from my floor. It took a few rides to get accustomed to the nauseating sensation of free falling on the way down, and being ejecting from a jet fighter on the way up.

The diverse variety of stores and restaurants along the perimeter of the lobby can be entered from the lobby or the street. The *StockBroker*, located on the top floor, is a members only club, exclusive to Wall Streeters like me. I've closed my share of deals there.

The common area of the lobby includes scattered pods of chairs and tables. Greenery, art exhibits, and sculptures of all shapes and sizes separate each pod, giving it an eloquent style. My favorite sculpture is the modern day remake of *The Thinker*. Except, instead of his hand holding up his chin, he's holding an iPad. The ceiling extends past the 20th floor, creating a spacious atmosphere.

Rasta drives a one-of-a-kind cab. It resembles a Jamaican flag on wheels. The dingy black tires without hubcaps complete the visual.

"Boss Man, good to see you again. Over to your lawyers we go."

"We've got plenty of time so take it slow. I've a deposition today from a prior deal. The extra time will help me rehearse my answers."

"No problem, Boss Man. I need to fuel up anyway. Tell me about your de-p-a-whatever. It's serious?"

"Just a formality. The Sperry kids missed out on buying their father's company because of their laziness. They've decided to seek treble damages instead of the settlement we offered. They contend Sperry signed an invalid power-of-attorney. He did not act in accordance with the Corporation's charter, rendering the sale void. Blah, blah, blah. They're just greedy bastards wanting more of the proceeds."

"Proceeds?"

"Cash, Rasta. That's all they care about. Cash and more cash."

"Ahh, I see. I'm going to stop there to fill up and make a quick call."

Rasta, short for Rastafarian has evolved into my personal cabbie. He's a master navigator and wastes no time getting me around. I pay him well, and let him drive one of my personal cars every now and then to keep him connected. You can tell a good cabbie by the dents he's accumulated over the years. If they're at the corners of the cab, he's good. If they're in the middle, stay away! I wonder if he knows my real name.

Rasta introduced me to my lawyer, Mark Stephens, four years ago. Mark's one of the best money can buy in New York. He majors in mergers and acquisitions with a minor in insider trading cover ups. His value as a lawyer far exceeds his value as a person; precisely why he succeeds at protecting investors like me. He's got two weaknesses, women and booze—I keep him well stocked with both.

"It'll be an hour or so," I told Rasta, "see you then."

I flicked a 20 over the seat. I got out watching as he sped off, darting in and out of oncoming traffic. I'm amazed his cab is still in one piece.

I took a deep breath and headed up to the *Dump*. This will be the last clean air I'll breathe for the next hour.

I waved to Joe, the owner of the building. He's also the proprietor of the rank dry cleaners located on the ground level directly below the dump. The steamy stench emitted from his patented process, combined with Mark's cheap cigar fumes, creates quite the aroma on floor number two.

"Good afternoon, Rich," Shelley said. "They're in his office waiting on you." She smiled, patting her big red hair back in place as I walked past. Her tight sweaters and short skirts resemble an out of work movie star posing as a business woman. Knowing Stephens' taste in women, it wouldn't surprise me. Her makeup s so thick she could remove it all in one piece and put it back on later. I returned her smile and entered Stephens' office ready for action.

The usual filth filled the tiny office. Files, newspapers, magazines, and decaying food wrappers from every eatery known to man were slung all over the tiny room. The cheap, white plastic trash cans decorated by permanent stains from unknown liquids overflowed with trash. The ashtrays look like mountains of volcanic ash with butts protruding from every angle. The excess ash created snow-like drifts along his desk top. The stench caused me to wretch.

On a positive note, it's a great place to bring the prosecution. There's no way for them to maintain concentration here.

His uptown office is the polar opposite. It's clean, quiet, and the staff conducts themselves in a professional manner. We handle all of our M&A business there. If we ever bought one of those clients to the *Dump* we'd be run out of town. Different meetings require different settings--we call it our home field advantage.

"Mr. Green," Tom Cromack said, "nice to see you again. I presume you're aware I represent the Sperry family and will be conducting the deposition today."

"Can we get on with it?" I asked.

"Sure, Mr. Green, whenever you're ready." He pulled a solid gold watch from his pocket, flipped it open, and shook his head. Putting it back into his pocket he said, "We've waited on you for 30 minutes. But if you're ready we can get started."

I respect Cromack's moxy, too bad he's on the wrong side.

"No objections from me. Let's get this over with. I've much more important things to do."

"Apparently," he mumbled under his breath.

After an eternity of basic questions and idle chat, designed as payback for making him wait, he got down to the crux of the matter.

"Mr. Green," he said, "did you have access to any written, spoken, or rumored communications of any sort that would be considered insider information under the appropriate penal codes of the State of New York? And if so, did you disclose as required?"

"You don't have to answer that, Rich," Stephens shook his head. "It's already on the record. And the judge ruled against any insider trading violations."

"Let me rephrase," Cromack said. "When did you find out about the apartment?"

"Which apartment?"

"How many did you get?"

"How many what?"

He lifted his hands in surrender. "Okay, the apartment located at Liberty Terrace, 380 Rectore Place Apt 24E. You know, the one in which you now live?"

"What about it?"

"When," he asked, "did you know of its existence?" He took a breath. "Before or after you made your offer? An offer that turned out to be 20% lower than the other qualified offers."

This guy knows something. I snuck a glance at Stephens while he twiddled his fingers and wiggled around in his chair.

"What's the relevance to this case, Cromack?" Stephens asked. "If you have new discovery, you must provide it before we continue. You know the rules."

"You signed for it over a week ago." He roamed the room with his eyes taking in the wretched mess. "How you operate in this pig sty's beyond me, but that's not my problem, is it boys."

He redirected his eyes on me, "Please answer the question."

Stephens tilted his head to the left gesturing for me to answer.

"I found out when everybody else d d. It had no relevance to my offer."

My underarms started getting moist.

"You sure?" he asked. "There's nothing you'd like to add?"

Stephens coached me with a slight head shake.

"Nope, I'm good."

"Okay, suit yourself. Looks like you leave no choice but to press on with our case. The family's upset about you stealing the company from them and will continue until they're satisfied."

"What will that take?" Stephens asked. "We already offered more than we should."

"They'd like their company back."

"You know that's impossible," Stephens said. "We're already acquitted of any wrong doing..."

"You weren't acquitted of anything," Cromack budded in. "The judge dismissed the case for lack of evidence. It could always be retried..."

"That a threat?" I asked standing up over him.

"Relax, Rich," Stephens said.

He grabbed me by the shoulder pressing me back into the chair.

"No threat, big boy, just saying he left the case open should someone want another shot at you."

"I agreed to pay the family a reasonable settlement, which they accepted, then rejected. What's their price now?"

"They're seeking treble damages, which compute to 4.5 million dollars. You have rejected this twice already.

"And I'll reject it again."

"I suggest we go in front of the judge and let him decide," Stephens said. "We'll agree to be bound by his decision. We're done here."

"I'll talk with them," Cromack winked and smiled, rising from his chair. "If we meet again, it'll be at my office, not in this God forsaken place. Good day, gentlemen."

He left the office shaking his foot trying to free up an old sandwich wrapper clinging to the bottom of his shoe.

I went to the window to verify he'd left and saw Rasta's cab parked across the street. It appeared as though they spoke, but I couldn't tell for sure. My view skewed by the solid layer of dust and grime covering the window panes. I turned away avoiding the sandwich wrappers heading out of the office.

"Where you going?" Stephens asked. "Shouldn't we discuss what happened?"

"Once we hear back from Cromack. My cab's here. I'm calling it a day."

I flew past Shelley's painted on smile heading down to the street.

"Ahh, Boss Man, how'd the de-p-a-whatever turn out?"

"Do you know the man who just left here?"

"No, why do you ask?"

"It looked like you spoke when he walked by."

"Oh, that man. He asked if I could drive him back to his office. I tell him no, I'm waiting on you."

"You sure you don't know him?"

"No, Boss Man, I don't know him."

I've trusted Rasta with sensitive information in the past. His exchange with Cromack bothers me. What are the chances they know each other in a city of 8 million people with just as many cabs?

"Bring me home."

Monday, August 22, 2010 4:00 PM
Rectore Street

Before Rasta left, I said, "I'm having dinner with Rosa tonight. I need to pick her up at 6:30. So swing back by here around 6."

"Okay Boss Man, no problem. Where you taking her?"

"Luke's, down by the financial district. I love that place."

"Very nice Boss Man. You two...you know?"

"I don't know. She asked me for once."

He dropped me at the curb. I shot up to my apartment on the 24th floor wondering what Rosa has in mind. Our custom calls for me to arrange our rendezvous. She initiated tonight, which means something exciting may happen.

My apartment came as an unexpected fringe benefit from our recent Sperry deal. We uncovered some juicy information from our informant about Joe Sperry. He bought the place under the pretense of business related housing for his distinguished vendors and suppliers. However, it's only inhabitants have been the harem of women he flew in to satisfy his lust. He had no problem including it in our deal in exchange for silence. Once the family found out about the apartment, they moaned about losing it. Once they found out why it existed, they went crazy. I don't blame them. There's no way I'm spilling my guts on this.

The balcony overlooks the Hudson River and the Esplanade creating a spectacular view, much better than Pine Street. Persuading Sperry to include the apartment in our deal seemed like a coup inside a coup, the deal of the century. Now, I have lawyers on my butt, unhappy heirs wanting more money, and some clown trying to cash in on my success. I'll be lucky to break even once it's settled.

I needed a shower to rid myself of the "dump" stench. My answering machine blinked indicating one new message.

"Rich, this is Rosa. Concerning this evening, I'd prefer to meet you at Luke's. No need to pick me up."

I didn't think much about her message until I got out of the shower. What does she mean "prefer" to meet me at Luke's? One word changes the whole context of her message. If she doesn't want me to pick her up, she may not want me to drop her off either.

Dr. Rosa Milano-Green and I met six years ago at a fundraiser for Attorney General Robert Pines, hosted by Rogers, Dean, and Rogers, my former employer. We talked on occasion, hitting it off big about three years ago. Our busy schedules prevented us from seeing too much of each other at first, which didn't work well. We decided to get married, hoping to lift our relationship to new heights, but that hasn't worked real well either. After 11 months we separated, but with her condition we're trying to reconcile our differences.

We've seen each other three times over the last two months. The first date ended without any crisis. Our second date lasted an entire weekend and provided plenty of fireworks. Our last date came to an abrupt end when she asked me about having children. I didn't like the question, and she hated my answer even more. We haven't spoken much since. My intuition tells me she's expecting more than our casual arrangement has provided.

I'll be donning my light beige shirt with blue floral print, a light blue undershirt, and white khaki pants. A festive pattern for a festive evening, I hope.

"Looking spiffy Boss Man. I've always known you're a Jamaican at heart."

"Bring me right to Luke's. Rosa will meet us there."

"Everything okay Boss Man?"

"I'll find out soon enough. Don't stray too far in case I need you."

"Yes sir." He cranked up his island jams and took off while I braced myself for possible impact. We arrived at Luke's in one piece.

"Don't be too far away," I reminded him. He waved and took off.

I arrived early, grabbed a table and ordered an Allagash Dubbel Reserve, my favorite beer. Luke's stocks it's coolers with Maine's finest micro brews to compliment their premium lobsters. Rosa will drink MBC's Peepers Pale Ale. They claim to donate 1% of every sale to non-profits of all kinds. Rosa gets sucked in by these gimmicks. She volunteers and provides medical care pro bono. I do nothing for free.

I slammed down the Reserve and ordered another along with Rosa's drink, and our food. We order the same dish every time, The Noah's Ark. It contains two shrimp rolls, two lobster rolls, and two crab rolls, along with four huge claws and chips. The top notch food and drink play second to the staff. They make this place special. Of all of Luke's locations, we like this one best.

Rosa arrived in her scrubs. She gave me a faint smile as she approached, sitting down at the counter next to me—no kiss, no hug. Her long auburn hair pulled tight in a ponytail extending down past her shoulder blades—and no makeup. Way out of character for her, unless she just came from surgery.

"Hi Rich. Been here long?"

"A few minutes. I drank one while I waited. No big deal."

"Did you order us the usual?"

"Of course. There aren't many options to choose from."

We sat quietly, paying more attention to the television than each other.

"How've you been? We haven't talked much since our last date."

"I'm good," she replied. "There's a reason we haven't talked much. Do you know what it is?"

"Instead of playing the game to see if I'm in touch with your feelings, just tell me what's wrong."

"The whole thing." Her sparkling hazel eyes became filled with anguish.

"The same life, the same food, and as you say 'not many options to choose from.' We need, or I need to spice things up. Move out of my comfort zone and explore new things."

"See other people?"

"Is that what you want?"

"No, of course not."

"You know what I'm talking about, Rich."

"Like acting married and having kids?" It came out with a cynical edge, not helping my cause any.

"Yes! Just like acting married and having kids. Maybe you think it's a joke, but I don't. I want a family, a house, a dog, and a life. I'm not getting any younger you know. And neither are you."

"Rosa, you're the perfect wife. And you'd be a great mother of our kids, But the timing's not right for me. There's too much going on, and I can't be distracted by kids, and..."

"A wife? Go ahead. Say it."

Okay, take a deep breath and think before you speak. This may be the last sentence we share as a couple. After a few seconds I went for it.

"Rosa, I love you, and would take you back as my wife today, if you'd agree. As for kids, I just don't see it anytime soon. I'm sorry. I don't want us to break up, I'm just not ready."

"Not ready for what? Commitment, love, happiness? Which one of these scares you the most, Rich?"

"I'm not scared of any of them."

"Then what's holding you back?"

We both sat there facing each other, afraid to make eye contact. She grabbed a shrimp roll and then slammed it back down on the plate, knocking it off the counter. The plate crashed onto the floor, and pieces shot everywhere as crab, shrimp, and lobster followed. Now we had everyone's attention. She started to cry while heading toward the door. I motioned to Storr, working behind the register I'll be right back and went after her.

"Rosa, wait," I yelled. "Hang on, don't leave. We can work it out."

"I don't think we can, Rich. I don't think we can," she said. "Leave me alone. I'll call you. We're not done with this yet." She hailed a cab and left.

"What do we need to finish?" I yelled as she took off.

I called Rasta while walking back into Luke's to pay and help clean up.

"Sorry, Storr," I said. "What do I owe you?"

"$63.45. Don't worry about the mess, I'll get it."

"Thanks." I gave him a $100 and waited until Rasta pulled up.

"Take me home. I need to be at the studio no later than 8:30 AM tomorrow. So pick me up around 7:30."

"What you got going on?"

"My monthly spot on Financial News Network."

Tuesday, August 23, 2010 9:00 AM
FNN Studio

"Game faces on. Let's go. In three--ready. Three, two, and. . . action."

The opening medley of music started blasting while the credits began scrolling across the bottom of the teleprompter. The Morning Edition is about to begin.

"Good Morning World. I'm Sarah Givens and you're watching The Morning Edition. Today my guest host for this segment is Rich Green, owner of Green Enterprises, one of the most respected and successful investors of our era."

She turned to me and said, "We've missed you the last few months. How've you been?"

"Never better, Sarah, thanks for asking."

"Before we get into what you're up to these days, Mike Franklin is standing by on the floor on the New York Stock Exchange. Mike, what have you got for us?"

While the feed came in from the NYSE, I watched the craziness unfold on set of the most watched business show in America. Hyper interns armed with headsets, clipboards, and caffeine flew around the studio screaming orders to each other. Each focused on their role, yet cognizant of what the others needed. Blinking LED lights, microphones, cameras, and monitors worked overtime trying to keep pace with the feeds coming in from the markets around the world.

"Places," someone shouted from the background, "15 seconds to showtime."

It's complete chaos until the director shouts his cue. Within seconds the madness converts into order, an amazing transformation to watch. I'm glad it's a part-time gig.

The timer behind the main camera worked its way down to five. Next to the timer some guy held up his hand. He counted with his fingers in unison to the timer. At zero he pointed at us and the show resumed.

I turned to Sarah, while also facing camera number 3. Sarah has a natural beauty requiring little make-up. Her long black hair, streaked with dark brown highlights, accents her Hispanic ethnicity. Her slender frame is well-defined evidence she spends a lot of time in the gym. She copyrights her semi-crooked smile.

"What exciting things are you working on these days?"

"All kinds of great stuff. Searching for value in an over-bought market is my primary focus of course. Not an easy task now-a-days."

"Any companies come to mind?"

"I'd stay away from the cyclicals right now. At the end of any business cycle, they're the first to feel the effect. For my personal portfolio, I still like Amazon and Apple. I own both of these. They both show the ability to maintain strong sales in all markets. I'm also holding t-bills and cash until the correction plays out."

"What about your business portfolio? Who do you like or dislike?"

"Well, Sarah, we're taking a serious look at two companies we feel offer great value. We can't disclose them at this time. If we decide to pursue one or both, you'll have the exclusive."

"Thanks, we're looking forward to it. So there's still value in today's market?"

"There's always value somewhere in the world!"

Sarah turned to the camera and said, "In our next segment, Rich will take questions from our viewing audience. Text or email your questions to the addresses listed on your screen. Morning Edition will return in a moment."

She turned toward me and we started smiling and talking about nothing while the camera faded out and switched to a commercial break. Sarah and I get along well enough to do the show. Off the air, we go our separate ways.

Sarah Givens, the premier business reporter on the nation's most respected network, Financial News Network. She gets things her way, all the time. I've learned to accept and use it to my advantage when possible. I prefer her as my ally. She buries her enemies.

"We're back with Rich Green, one of the country's foremost investors, founder and President of Green Enterprises."

The camera zoomed in and I smiled, "Great to be here, Sarah."

"Before we get to the viewer's questions, I have one for you."

"Shoot."

"Is it true you're a big supporter of Attorney General Robert Pines' campaign for Governor?

"Yes. AG Pines is a solid man with great integrity. He has our best interest at heart."

"When you say 'us' do you mean big business, or his constituency?"

"Both. Pines understands both sides, and he'll be the best Governor New York has had in quite some time."

She turned away from me, faced the camera, and after a brief pause said, "I think you'll find a lot of others disagree, but that's why we vote."

Another pause and crooked smile for effect.

"Okay, G.T. In Nebraska has our first question," Sarah announced. "With all the leg work required to buy a company, how do you handle it all with only a handful of employees?"

"Great question G.T.," I said. "To be exact, I only have one full-time employee. There are many fantastic companies who specialize in the M & A arena doing the work I cannot or do not want to handle. I sub-contract these duties to them. This way, I'm not bogged down with hiring and laying off during peaks and valleys in the economic cycles. Not all of my peers agree with this arrangement, but it works for me, and that's all I'm concerned about."

Sarah nodded her head in approval. There's a first time for everything.

"Next question. H.L., also from Nebraska asks, 'what signs do you look for to help you determine what companies to buy?' Good question," she added.

"A great question," I said. "Sarah, I'll answer it in two parts. First, we have to verify they're worth more than the current market price. If not, I move on. If so, we explore many other areas. Market share, management, pipeline of products, cash on hand, and of course debt. The most important reason though is why. Why do they want to sell? If I can fix the issue or solve the problem, they're in play."

"B.S. from Newark, New Jersey has our last question of the day. He asks, 'I've been following you a long time and never understood why you'd buy a company just to rip it apart. Can you explain why you do this?'"

I sat back and took a sip of water before attempting to tackle the question.

"Well, that's a tough question to answer. Much tougher in a tight economy with high unemployment we're facing now. Many companies grow and expand trying to develop what they call, economies of scale. They try to lower cost, gain market share, and increase profits. However, only a few ever succeed at this. Most end up in a bureaucratic mess and become dinosaurs. They can't function with the speed and agility they once enjoyed. They start losing their value and the stockholders become restless. I come in with a solid solution. I buy them at a discount, break them up, and sell the pieces, hopefully for a profit."

I took another drink, a deep breath, and was about to continue, but Sarah jumped in.

"What about the employees of those companies who gave their life, and then just like that," she snapped her fingers, "It's over."

I took another drink and fired back.

"I perform a function the market needs. A cleansing of the weak, if you will."

Looking right into Sarah's eyes I continued, "Before you interrupt, hear me out. Efficient markets only work when strong companies stay strong. The weak companies have three choices. Get stronger, get bought, or get taken out."

I went too deep, leaving no choice but to continue down this controversial path.

"The employees of these companies do not always suffer. Many times they stay with the companies and prosper under the new ownership. Other times jobs are lost. It's a cold and unfortunate truth, but it's reality. They'd lost them anyway once the company went under. Someone's gonna step in and profit, why not me?"

"Anything else before we wrap it up?" Sarah asked.

"Yes--one more thing. The owners of these companies should be blamed. They're the ones causing the problems by exerting poor leadership and management. I just clean up their mess. Some investors buy companies for long-term growth, some buy them for synergies. I buy broken companies, tear them apart, and sell off the pieces. That's what I do and I'm not ashamed of it."

The studio went silent. Sarah, as she does so well, broke the silence with unique poise and style.

"Well that about wraps it up for this segment." She turned to me, "Thanks to Rich Green for being here and sharing his innermost thoughts with us. As usual we enjoyed your insight and outspokenness."

"Thanks for having me," wondering if the entire world can see my nervousness.

The cameras faded out again as we left the stage. She swiveled and headed right while I headed left. She circled in front of the stage and headed toward me.

"Rich, hold on a moment."

I stopped, bracing myself for a verbal onslaught.

"I'm excited about your return to the show." She smiled catching me by surprise.

"Thanks, me too." My curiosity peaked.

"There's talk about expanding your role, if you're interested."

"Even after my tirade? I'm sure the hate mail will be flying in."

"I hope so. Even though I don't agree with your methods, it's nice to have someone who speaks their mind. Our station needs more of that. I'm tired of all the hyperbole and garbage we generate."

She stunned me with her frankness.

"Of course I'm interested, what do you have in mind?"

"A half-hour segment airing once a week on mergers and acquisitions—your specialty. If it's a success we can expand it to an hour. It'll be a great opportunity for you."

"I'd love to! Why me though?"

"We like your style and integrity. Plus you look good in front of the camera and not afraid to speak your mind. My producer, Sharon, will contact you in a few days to arrange a meeting. Until then...Ciao!" She smiled and walked by me toward her dressing room.

I stood there in shock. My own show—and a smile?

Tuesday, August 23, 2010 11:30 AM
FNN Studio

Rasta picked me up from the studio. We headed downtown to meet up with Ty.

"How'd it go Boss Man?"

"Great, I may even get my own show."

"Nice!"

"Yeah, well, we'll see."

I settled into the back seat focusing on my meeting this afternoon. What's his game? I shot Ty a text telling him to meet me in front of Stuart's, the other private lounge in my building.

"You okay back there, Boss Man?"

"Yeah, I'm fine, just thinking."

"About?"

"Just things, nothing in particular."

"We have 10 minutes Boss Man, maybe I can help you."

"I'm okay Rasta. Thanks anyway."

In the past I'd have talked to him about any issue without thinking twice. For now, I'll keep to myself.

"Suit yourself Boss Man. I'll drop you off and be back at 2:30. Call me if you need me sooner."

I got out and headed through the lobby straight to Stuart's. A beer would do me wonders right now. I sat down and ordered a Paulaner Salvator. A full bodied double bock imported from Munich, one of my favorites. Ty didn't respond to my text so I called him.

"Ty, I'll be in Stuart's, text me when you get here so I can get you in."

The Salvator hit the spot so well, I ordered another and called Ty again. This time he answered.

"Don't you return calls anymore?"

"Something came up. I'll never make it down there by 1:00 pm. Can we just meet uptown?"

I looked at the phone amazed.

"What do you mean something came up? We're talking about our business. Get your butt down here."

"I'll never make it down there in time, but I'll be watching you. We'll meet at Starbucks as planned."

I didn't even respond. I hung up and slammed down beer number two. What could be more important than this?

The first two beers made me light headed, so I ordered a sandwich with Salvator number three. Stuarts packs in business folk searching for a quiet place to spend their afternoons. They act like they're conducting deals, but in reality they are hiding from their jobs. Slamming drinks to reduce the pressures the Street dishes out. Stuarts ranks near the top of the list for the singles crowd. A lot of that goes on as well.

At this time of the day, the flat screens show either FNN or ESPN. I parked myself at the bar watching the stock market take a beating. FNN reports the Dow Jones dropped 500 points, and the S&P lost 49. Huge losses for each index. I hope this isn't indicative of what's about to transpire uptown.

I sipped number three, and took my time with the ham and Swiss club. Once 2 PM rolled around I text Rasta and went outside to meet him.

"Where's your partner Boss Man?"

"He's meeting me there, bring me to NASDAQ."

"Got it!"

Driving in the Big Apple is unpredictable to say the least. A half-hour drive can turn into an all day affair. Servants like Rasta make this city work. Even though I'm suspicious of him, I appreciate his navigation skills on days like today.

I called Ty. After four rings it went to voicemail. He'd better be there!

As we pulled in front of NASDAQ, I got out, "Pick us up at the Starbucks across the street."

I love this city and all the craziness it brings. It inspires me like nothing else. A city built for winners like me. This city has atmosphere. The multitude of various noises combines to form a steady hum. The relentless crowds perform their daily pursuit to get ahead of each other. All this can overwhelm outsiders, but they lift my spirits making me feel strong.

Today however, facing a brisk, stiff wind, the sun hidden by the grayish clouds, I stand alone at the curb, petrified. My accuser may be any one of the thousands swarming Times Square today.

Scanning the ocean of people trying to spot Ty proved impossible. I'd all but given up when a slight poke in the back startled me.

"Don't turn around," a familiar voice said. "This is not a hold-up."

I froze.

"Listen carefully Green, from now on you'll refer to me as Mr. X."

"Okay Mr. X," I answered.

"I know about your dealings with Sperry. I also know about three other times you used inside information to make a killing."

"And?"

"You made a fortune breaking the law and screwing other people. From now on we're a team, and I call the shots."

"I work alone."

"Not anymore."

"No dice pal." I tried to act confident, but started trembling. I closed my eyes and took a deep breath, hoping to regain stability. "How about I walk away. We'll pretend this never happened."

"Go ahead, walk away. See what happens."

"What do you want?"

"I'm going to hand you a card with a website on it. It'll give you all the information you need on your next takeover. Or, should I say, our next takeover. I'll be monitoring your activity on the site for the next 48 hours. If you do not access it by this time tomorrow, you can kiss your freedom goodbye. Do you understand?"

"Yes I do."

"I thought you might. Here's the card. Don't turn around. I'll be in touch."

As I took the card from his weathered hand, I noticed the ring on his finger. It looked familiar, like a college ring. I waited a few seconds before turning around hoping to catch a visual of Mr. X. Instead I saw thousands of people scurrying like rats searching for cheese. They call New York the "melting pot" for good reason. Every race, creed, and religion is represented, and represented well.

Maybe Ty caught a glimpse. I dialed his cell, but it went straight to voicemail. This city has everything except good cell phone reception.

"Ty, call me," I said. "Did you see him? Call me back. I'm headed to Starbucks."

I crossed the street and made my way through the crowd hoping to find Ty. It's always packed in here. If we're in a recession, nobody told the coffee drinkers. They're out in full force today. I can't even get inside. I'm amazed at the resilience of their business model. Who'd have thought coffee could be this important to so many people. Maybe Mr. X will get some dirt on these guys.

I grabbed a cold drink and waited in line. I crack up listening to the ordering dialogue. I don't play the double latte, half frappe, and lightly shaken not stirred game. For me it's a cold drink or a medium coffee with cream and sugar.

I went back outside and called Ty. It went straight to voice mail again, and I hung up and called Rasta to come get me.

I jumped into the Jamaican flag on wheels and headed back to my office. I called Ty a few more times with the same result. He'd better have a great explanation for blowing me off.

"What's up Boss Man, you don't seem real happy."

"I'm not. Ty hasn't returned my calls. He knew how important this is to me."

"I'm sure he's got a good explanation, Boss Man. He'll call."

"He better."

The high-potency beer and meeting Mr. X took its toll on me.

"Wake me up when we get back to my office."

"Okay Boss Man."

I closed my eyes, hoping to wake up from this miserable dream. Instead Rasta's voice invaded my sleep, "We're here Boss Man. Need me anymore today?"

"Pick me up at 6."

Off he went like a mad man in a demolition derby.

I took a similar approach through the lobby. Dodging and weaving through the crowd on my way to the VIP elevators. I almost made it without incident until I crashed head-on with a young woman. The impact sent her flying backward, her coffee spewing from her mug, drenching her from head to toe. Her cell phone dislodged itself from her hand, landing in the fountain behind her. A cold silence filled the lobby...until she got up.

"What's wrong with you? Why don't you watch where you're going, jerk!" Her squeal echoed throughout the entire lobby. This must have awoken the security guards and they came running over to investigate.

"You okay, Mr. Green?" The dumpy one said.

"You're worried about him?" Her voice shrieked to an octave level seldom reached by humans. "What about me? He ran me over you buffoon. Look at my new outfit--he ruined it and you ask if he's okay? Where's my phone?"

"Sorry, ma'am, " he answered.

"You will be sorry if you don't help me find my phone."

Good thing this isn't a real emergency.

"It's in the fountain young lady," I replied. "I'm sorry about this."

I pulled out my wallet. "Here's my card and $100. Please send me the bill for the rest. I'll take care of it."

"Do you know how much this outfit cost?" She stood with her hands on her hips bobbing her head like a rooster.

"And, what about my phone? This measly hundred dollars doesn't even cover my shoes."

I don't need this today. My tension started rising.

"I don't care about your pretty little outfit; what your shoes cost, or what you do about a phone. I told you I'll take care of it. I'm in a hurry, send me the bill."

"Next time watch where you're going mister."

"Next time don't walk, text and drink coffee at the same time. Or you may get yourself killed."

She continued her attitude as walked off toward the elevator. I half-way expected a shoe or something flying at me from behind, but I made it to the elevators unscathed.

The VIP elevator blasted me up to the 55th floor in seconds. I straightened up my clothes as I walked by BQE to get a sneak preview of our future Miss Americas. Before swiping my keycard I noticed movement through the sculptured glass window in the door. Someone's in my office.

Tuesday, August 23, 2010 3:30 PM
Pine Street

The electronic mechanism securing my office generates an audible click as it unlocks. I took a deep breath and swiped my card slowly to keep the element of surprise on my side. Within a split second of unlocking, I burst through the door and tackled my uninvited visitor.

We crashed into the coffee table between the reception desk and couch. The collector edition books, cheap candy dish, and expensive antique wooden schooner flew across the room. The books and candy dish survived without damage. The sailboat shattered as it hit the wall behind us.

"What the heck, man?" Ty managed to grunt as we slid along the hardwood floor.

I got up and dusted myself off before helping Ty to his feet. Aside from the fact he absorbed the full force of a viscous blindside tackle, he just cost himself a few hundred dollars for the model.

"What are you doing in my office? More importantly, where were you this afternoon?"

I gave him no time to respond before continuing my interrogation.

"What's wrong with you?" I studied him up and down. "You look terrible."

Under normal circumstances, Ty keeps himself well groomed--almost to the point of being obsessive. Not so today--something's wrong. His shoulder length black hair, normally slicked back into a ponytail, hung loose covering his ears. Strands of random hair straggled away from his head giving him an electrified look.

I haven't slept much the last few nights," he said. "I think I'm being followed."

"You're being what?"

"Followed. Someone's following me."

"Why would anyone follow you?"

He returned my verbal sarcasm with the "go screw yourself" look I've grown accustomed to. I noticed the deep bags under his bloodshot eyes.

"You sure you're not becoming more paranoid?"

"I'm not sure about anything at the moment. Someone in a green car has been tailing me since Monday. I didn't want him following me to Times Square, so I went to Central Park instead."

"Nobody's following anyone, Ty. Why didn't you answer your phone? I called you a million times."

"I left it in the cab. They're sending the driver over to return it."

"The lost phone excuse, huh?" My tension started to climb again. I took a breath to calm down.

"When did you get here?"

"Two minutes before you tackled me." He looked toward the wall where my prize ship lay in pieces. "Sorry about the ship."

"I'll give you the dealer's number so you can replace it."

We walked into my office from the reception area leaving the mess behind. The entire north side of the 55th floor belongs to me; six-thousand square feet of prime space of which I occupy a small portion. It came with the InCahoots deal. All in all, there are nine offices, three conference rooms, and four private restrooms.

Upon taking ownership of the offices, I hired the best designer in New York to give it a much needed facelift. She furnished the reception area with expensive antiques. The desk, coffee table, and end tables are a matching set. The light brown oak finish still looks pristine even though it's over 60 years old. The couch and executive wingback chairs date to 1950. They needed attention and now match perfect.

The three original oil paintings depict scenes of old kitchens complete with colorful fruit baskets, wood burning ovens, and iron pot racks suspended from the rustic ceilings. These paintings enhance the colors of the furniture, bringing coziness to the room.

Six original Seth Thomas mantle clocks of varying sizes ring on the hour in 15 second intervals. The strategic placement blends their unique pitches and tones into a symphony of bells and gongs.

The decor in my office creates a sailor's paradise. Large festive prints of the islands accent the aquamarine tinted walls. Framed original sailing maps dating back to the 1800's hang next to the print of the waters they once navigated.

My prize possession is the salt water aquarium spanning the entire east wall opposite of my desk. I fall into a trance watching the pastel orange clown fish interact with the multi-finned yellow and orange dotted cardinal. The scribbled angelfish, Chico, is my favorite. His translucent blue and black fins create the base for his brilliant fluorescent yellow tail and stripe wrapped around its midsection—a beautiful fish.

Ty sat in the crushed leather recliner as usual.

"Tell me about the green car," I asked.

"I first noticed it Monday afternoon on my way home. For some reason it caught my eye. I saw it again Tuesday morning on my way uptown. I didn't see it again until I headed home for the evening. My driver took an alternate route home, and he followed us the entire way. I got out to try and stop him, but he turned before I could get to him."

I thought about who may want to follow Ty.

"Maybe Mr. X had you followed. This way he could insure I came alone."

"Who?"

"Oh, that's right. You missed our meeting. Mr. X; the guy you were supposed to help me with today."

He didn't appreciate my condescending tone, but I didn't care at this point.

"Regardless of who it is, it spooks me."

"Did they follow you here?"

"I didn't see them on the way back. I took the precaution of walking the last few blocks."

"I'm sure it's nothing. If you see them again call me."

"I wish they'd return my phone soon. I'm lost without it."

I signed on to my computer and went to "isitwindyinchicago.com" to fulfill my requirement and see what Mr. X had in store for me.

"You haven't asked about my meeting yet," I said. "Did you forget we're in business?"

"Sorry, my mind wandered off. What happened?"

I clicked through the first few pages until a profile for a company called Jenkins and Jenkins loaded on the screen.

"Well other than blackmailing me to work with him, and threatening me if I didn't. Not much."

"What's your problem today?" he asked.

"Excuse me?"

"Nothing, forget it."

"I'm not going to forget it. You let me down big today. What if this clown wanted to hurt me?"

He lowered his head avoiding eye contact.

"Are you with me, Ty? If you're not I need to know now."

"I'm with you, Rich."

My office phone rang and Ty rushed to grab it.

"Hello," he said. "Yes, it is." After a few seconds passed he continued. "Okay, I'll be down, Thanks."

I leaned back in my chair expecting his explanation.

"My phone, they're downstairs with my phone" he said, and rushed out of the office.

I went to Edgars.com and pulled up the 10K on Jenkins to start the process. Mr. X provided the ammo, it's up to us to find the gun. I spent the better part of an hour reviewing the financials on Jenkins when I realized Ty hadn't returned. I dialed his cell.

"Dude! Where'd you run off to now?"

"I'm taking care of a few things," he said. "What's up?"

"What do you mean, what's up! I'm running a business here, hello! We just talked about it. Remember?"

"Yes I remember. Jenkins and Jenkins, right?"

"You plan on working this with me? Or do you have more important things to do?"

"Give me the rest of the day to put out these fires. I promise I'll be ready to do my part."

"Be here at 0900 tomorrow. No excuses. I don't care if you're followed, lose your phone, or an arm. You better be here!"

I hung up and watched Chico glide unabated through the tank. He has it made, even the big, bad bamboo shark shows his respect.

Wednesday, August 24, 2010 9:30 AM
Rectore Street

The time has come to lay down the law with Ty before getting started on Jenkins. Although, I'd prefer to have him with me, I'm prepared to go it alone. He's either engaged or gone.

"Six PM tonight, Boss Man?" Rasta asked as we pulled up in front of my office.

"Not sure. Keep your phone handy."

He waved and darted out into traffic without hesitation. I took the opposite approach today walking through the lobby slow and deliberate. There's no need to repeat yesterday's chaos. I stepped into the supersonic elevator and rocketed up to my floor. BQE opens at 10, so I took the shorter route to my office, right across the hall from the elevator.

I started the coffee maker, fed the fish, logged on to Edgars.com, and dialed into my office voicemail.

"Richie, my man. It's Jack. I got a few ideas to run by you. Call me so we..." I deleted it before he finished.

"Rich, Mark here. Cromack called and wants to meet. Says the family wants a quick settlement. Call me at the uptown office tomorrow." I hit delete again.

The squealing hinges on the entry door came to life. I leaned back as Ty trudged in to my office.

"What now?" I asked him. "You look worse than yesterday." The salt and pepper facial hair sprouted from all directions matching the intensity of his frayed black mane.

"Same clothes as yesterday?"

"No sleep," he said. "But I'm here and ready to work."

"Followed again? Or do you have a new tragedy today?"

"I'd appreciate some understanding every now and then. Your coldness gets old."

"Sorry, I've less than 24 hours to figure this whole thing out. There's no time to be all warm and mushy. Can we get started?"

"What did Jack want?"

He's trying my patience right now.

"He wants to get together to discuss some ideas. He's tried to team up with me for over a year now. And I ..."

"We should bring him on," he interrupted me. "He's always got something working."

"I can't be distracted by a wanna-be big shot right now. He's a pain. Right in the you know where. If you'd like to join him..."

"I thought you got along, that's all I'm saying."

"Tolerate. He and Stephens... two of a kind. Jack brings nothing to the table. At least Stephens provides some value. Now, can we get started, or do you have other objections?"

"No more objections your honor," he said.

"Based on the information Mr. X provided, Jenkins can be bought and split into three separate companies. We could make a killing on this deal."

"Really, how do we begin?"

"By following the steps he outlined on the website."

I continued reading the page on my monitor.

"He's got it all laid out. A nice package."

"What do you know about them as a company?" Ty asked.

"What?"

"You know, what do you know about them?"

"Nothing much at the moment. Does it matter? Soon we'll know more about those jokers than they know about themselves."

There's something up with Ty. I sense a heavy conflict inside. I can't identify it yet, but I'll have my answer soon. I dialed Stephens and put him on speaker.

"Hey Rich, what's going on?" his scratchy voice came through the speaker.

"Ty and I want to discuss our new project with you." I made sure he knew of Ty's presence.

"Did you get my message about Cromack?" Stephens asked.

"Yes, I did. Put it to rest for me, but do not pay anymore than we've already offered. If they refuse, tell them we'll see them in court. Got it?"

"I got it."

"Good, next I need you to file forms 3 and 4 with the SEC. I'm going after a company called Jenkins and Jenkins. Ticker symbol of JNKS. They're on the NASDAQ. Current price--$12.20. Put our limit order in at $12.25 and start buying all the way up to $14.00."

"Your new deal?" he asked.

"Yes. Should be another slam dunk for us."

"How'd you hear about them?"

"I'll bring you up to speed tomorrow. In the meantime get moving."

"I'll get right on it. Should I enlist Hornesby for this one?"

"No, we can't afford any surprises like Sperry. Your guy missed the power of attorney conflict, costing us about 2 million dollars. You did fire him, right?"

"Worse. He's working my insurance fraud cases." His sinister laugh came through the speaker followed by hacking and coughing.

"Move fast on Sperry, and faster on Jenkins. Call me when you file the forms so I can pay them a visit. I want both of these done by the end of the year. I'm having a new PI coming by my office this afternoon. He comes highly recommended."

"Who'd you hire?" Stephens asked.

"We'll talk about it later, gotta go." End call.

We retain a team of private investigators for these assignments. They're devious, sly, and understand discretion--in most cases. Their latest mistake cost me a fortune. I'll never use them again.

Reef Stantchin is new to the scene. I'm told if there's a skeleton, he'll find it. We'll soon see.

He's been following Ty for three weeks, but doesn't drive a green car.

Wednesday, August 24, 2010 2:30 PM
Pine Street

Reef buzzed me from the guest phone inside the VIP elevator. I entered the code on my keypad authorizing his access to my floor. Within seconds he appeared in the hallway.

Gunnar "Reef" Stantchin grew up in Jersey with a background similar to most PI's--special Op's military training. There's no weapon he can't disassemble, reassemble, and fire with marksman like accuracy. He's a certified black belt in mixed martial arts, giving him a solid one-two punch. Glad he's on my team.

I escorted him through the reception area into my office, pointing to the plush leather chair on the side of my desk. He stands about three inches taller than me, putting him around 6'2". He handed me his grey silk sport coat revealing two things; a black long sleeve sweater magnifying his chiseled physique, and a dark metal pistol. He wears his light blonde hair slicked back, and sports a neatly trimmed van dyke, a tough, but good looking dude.

"Thanks for coming on such short notice. I have another job for you."

"What do you got?"

I went over the phone call, my meeting with Mr. X, and the website.

"I need you to find this clown. All I know about him is his hand had wrinkles and a class ring of some type. Maybe the website can help?"

"I'm already on it," Reef said. "You'll be happy to know I have photos of your Mr. X."

"How did you manage that?"

"We're following Ty like we're supposed to. However, when he decides to go uptown instead of with you I figure someone needs to watch your back. So my partner and I split, and I take a cab over to Times Square."

I sat back in my chair and stared at him in amazement. How'd he know?

"Since we're on a surveillance mission, I had my camera and snapped off a bunch of pictures of the two of you. He's smart though. He covered his face so most of the pictures won't help."

"Crap!"

Reef smiled a grin from ear to ear.

"Come on, Rich, I'm better than that."

"What do you mean?" I leaned toward him. My anticipation started to rise.

"I followed him by cab until he took off his coverings. I got close enough for some great pictures of his face. And better yet, found out where he went. I'll have a complete rundown by tomorrow noon."

"Did you bring the pictures with you?"

"Of course."

One by one we examined the pictures. I didn't recognize him at all.

"You're the absolute best!" I said to him and gave him a fist pump. "What do I owe you?"

"It's my job," he said. "I need to get moving. I'll assign my best hacker on the site to see what he can find. He should do it from your computer though. He's smart. He'll be monitoring who accesses the site."

"Good call, when can he get started?"

Thursday, August 25, 2010 10:00 AM
Pine Street

After a sleepless night and stressful morning, it's time to get in gear. I sat behind my desk and watched Chico. He didn't move an inch. He sat there suspended in the water staring at me. I wondered how much energy he expends keeping himself still. He doesn't appear to be moving, but he must be. Otherwise the current, however slight would carry him one way or another. Sort of like life, we're moving toward or away from our target and we don't even realize it at times. I dialed Mark Stephens.

"Good morning Rich," he said sounding half dead; like I felt.

"You alright, Mark? You're not sounding so good."

"Long night. You know how it is."

With him I try not to imagine, but I play along.

"Who is she?" We both laughed. "And will she see you again?" We laughed some more.

"I don't know, and I don't know." His sinister laugh echoed through my office, followed by his patented coughing and hacking. At this pace, he won't live long, but he'll enjoy every minute of his perverted life.

"Hey Mark, I've asked Reef Stantchin, my new PI, to join us. You on the line, Reef?"

"I'm here Rich. Good to know you, Mark?"

"Hey Reef, your guy came by last night and picked up my laptop. Have you heard from him yet?"

"He worked on it all night. He told me the website is encrypted quite well. He may not..."

"What are you guys talking about?" Stephens asked talking over Reef.

"The Jenkins deal. I had the pleasure of meeting my new extortionist, Mr. X on Tuesday. He's trying to muscle in on my business."

"Umm, okay," Stephens said.

"Says he's got dirt on me from our last few deals. I follow his lead, or he turns me in."

"And he suggested Jenkins?"

"Yep, I'm playing along until we find out who he is. Then we'll see who's leading who."

"Mr. X, huh. He couldn't come up with anything better than that?" Stephens asked. "Sounds cliche."

"We'll find him," Reef added.

"Jenkins developed a new technology they're releasing soon," I said. "X predicts this to be a monumental event. He's expecting this to add at least 20% more market share, positioning them as the leaders in brake systems for trucks and cars. As far as background and management, what do you have for me Reef?"

"CEO Steve Kemp and CFO Ralph Longo have a long history together. Longo referred Kemp five years ago. The board voted him in, even though Mr. Jenkins protested it. They've done a fair job of running the company. They've done a great job pilfering it."

"He shows Longo's gambling issues on the website. What's Kemp's story?" I asked him.

"He's busy buying and selling company stock under an alias of Johnny Jeffries. He's made hundreds of thousands of dollars playing his game. Longo wanted in, but Kemp refused. Now they're stalemated with dirt they can't use on each other. I'd call their current relationship adversarial, at best."

"What's the dirt on Longo?"

"The gambling problem."

"Okay, but many people have gambling problems."

"Not funded from the company coffers."

I nodded. I'm getting the picture.

"To the tune of several hundred thousand dollars," Reef continued. "Then comes the drinking and fooling around. The two make quite a pair."

Of course they do, otherwise they wouldn't be in this predicament. Their poor choices and lack of discipline will open the door for us to walk right in and buy their company before they know what hit them. The only wildcard here is Mr. X.

"Who's the least likely to put up a fight?" Stephens asked.

"Longo. His life's already in ruins. One more scandal and he'll just retire and drink himself to death. Kemp, on the other hand, is considered a pillar of strength in his family and church."

Typical church going hypocrite, spend Sunday acting like a saint and the rest of the week like Satan.

"So if I could convince Kemp to sell the company, he can make Longo a sweet deal to go away; they both win," I said. "What about the board? Will there be any resistance from them?"

"I'm still working on that," Reef said. "We'll have more answers by end of the week."

This guy's awesome. I don't know how I operated without him. I'd hate to have him poking around in my business.

"What about Ty?" I asked him. "What kind of mess has he gotten himself into?"

"Well, he has a mistress uptown, Mary, and his wife suspects as much. He led us there Tuesday afternoon. My guy says he only went inside for a few minutes before they came out arguing. They stood there on the steps of her building for ten minutes before he jumped in a cab and left."

"I hate liars. He made up a story about being followed so he went to Central Park instead of backing me up."

"He didn't lie about that," Reef said. "His wife hired a low rate private eye who drives a green car."

"The green car," I said. "It has him spooked."

"He's hanging with a guy named Bill Kaufmann," Reef added. "You know him, right?"

"Yeah, the three us worked together at Rogers."

"That's what I thought."

Nice, he's checking me out like he should.

"Anything else before I go?"

"Yes, one more thing. Check Ty's financial situation for me. See if he's in trouble. Otherwise, you've earned your pay in a big way, thanks Reef. Mark, stay on the line."

I heard Mark talking in the background and a door close.

"What's up Rich?" Stephens asked.

"You alone?"

"What do you mean?"

"I mean, is there someone in the room with you?"

"No, I'm alone."

"Mark, I heard a voice and a door close after Reef hung up."

"I'm alone, Rich. Promise."

He's playing games with me. There's someone with him.

"I hope so, if not, that's a huge breach of my privacy, Mark."

He didn't respond.

"Did you file the forms on Jenkins?" I asked him.

"Yes, I should get acceptance by tomorrow. Go ahead and set your appointment."

"What's our stock position?"

"We're up to 375,000 shares, and a 5 percent minority owner. The stock trades thin. Most shares held by board members and the Jenkins family trust."

"We'll talk later." I hung up.

Ty has become a major liability to me. Now Stephens gives me equal concern. I'd fire both of them on the spot, if I trusted they'd go away without causing me harm.

Thursday, August 25, 2010 2:15 PM
Pine Street

"Rich, Reef here, do you have a minute?"

"Yeah sure, what do you have for me?"

"About Ty," he said. "I have the information you requested this morning."

"Tell me what you have."

"For starters, his mistress "Mary" is married--and pregnant. We haven't verified the father yet, but Ty acts as though it's him. Only DNA can prove it one way or another."

"What else?"

"He's hurting financially. He's maxed out his cards and just refinanced his house. His savings and checking overdrawn. All in the last three months."

"Blackmail?"

"I'd be surprised," he answered. "She's loaded and doesn't need the money."

"Do you know what's causing this?"

"He withdrew the money in large amounts. Nothing we can trace. Maybe drugs, gambling . . ."

"I've known Ty for years and he's not a druggie or gambler."

"What about her? He's scared she'll roll over on him if he doesn't keep her supplied."

"Do you have proof?"

"Just a hunch, Rich. We're still checking around. We've also interviewed the other private eye and put the fear of God in him. Told him to report whatever he finds to us first or he'll regret it."

"I'll confront Ty next time I see him. He better shoot straight with me."

"Be easy on him."

"Why?"

"We all fall short, Rich."

I had no idea what he meant by his last statement.

"What about the website?"

"We couldn't trace it back to anything meaningful. He's monitoring access. He sent you a message telling you not to trace him, it's futile."

"Do you agree?"

"Websites can be tricky to trace, but remember we have pictures and a known location. He doesn't know we're all over him. I'll call you later. Take care."

"Thanks, you too."

I walked to the window and stared over the horizon. My cell buzzed.

"Hello."

"Mr. Green, I have your laptop ready."

"Thanks Lou, I'll meet you in the lobby at 5." End call.

I walked back to my desk and rehearsed my approach and the answers I expected from Ty in return. I punched his number on the speaker phone. If he doesn't come clean he's done. I have no time for these antics.

We play our game on the edge with no room for error, especially from poor judgment in our personal lives. Ty's finances and cheating, Mr. X, and Rasta's conversation with Cromack spell trouble. Rosa wanting to settle down seems minor in relation.

"Yeah Rich, what's up?"

"We need to talk today. When can you be here?"

"What about?"

"Many things. When can you be here?"

"About 45 minutes or so?"

"No later than. And Ty. . ."

"Yes, I'll be there. Relax."

Thursday, August 25, 2010 3:00 PM
Pine Street

Ty walked through the squeaky door--on time. A good start for what's to become a critical conversation.

"Ty, come back to the conference room. Turn your phone off. We don't need any interruptions."

My conference room has an eloquent, yet basic decor. Instead of Caribbean prints, I have photos of my heroes, Warren Buffet and Adam Smith, hanging along the wall running lengthwise of the room. Autographed photos cover the far wall. The two I'm most proud of; 43, and soon to be governor, Robert Pines, hang behind my chair. Eleven other dark brown leather chairs outline the fifteen foot oblong conference table. A stocked wet bar sets in one corner and a bathroom at the other. The window opposite the Warren Buffet wall overlooks the Hudson River.

Ty grabbed a chair facing the windows.

"Everything okay?" he asked knowing full well it isn't.

"I don't know yet," I said. "Why don't you start at the beginning. Tell me what's going on."

He cupped his hand over his mouth and rubbed his nose using his thumb and index finger.

"Well?" I asked. "Do you want to start, or should I help you along?"

"I'm not sure what you know."

"Does it matter what I know?"

We exchanged stares.

"Look Ty, I pay you damn well and expect you to carry yourself in a manner that doesn't bring unwanted attention to our business. You're acting reckless, at best."

He twisted his mouth to the right.

"All right, here goes." He released the locking mechanism on his chair putting it in full recline mode.

"A few months ago we met at the grille for lunch and a woman kept staring at me. Remember?"

"Yes, you kept telling me about her. Go on."

"Well, instead of leaving after you, I stayed behind and introduced myself to her. Well, one thing led to another. Now, I'm stuck with a pregnant mistress."

"And?"

"And she claims it's mine, but I'm not sure. When I arrived to pick her up for a paternity test, she refused. Now, she's threatened to tell Barbara."

"Who already knows..."

He looked at me, cocked his head, and squinted his eyes.

"She suspects. How did you..."

"The green car? Barbara hired a private investigator to follow you. Reef's guy caught up with him and put a scare into him."

"Reef?"

"My new PI."

"He's following me too, I take it."

"Yes, three weeks now. And good thing because he went to Times Square when you didn't show and has a bead on Mr. X."

"What else do you know?"

"You're a financial mess," I said piercing his eyes with mine. "Looks like your funding someone's habit."

He took a deep breath. "Barbara's talking about moving out. And, as if that's not enough, I'm dealing with a blackmailer. So yes, I'm a mess. I'm screwed--in every way."

"Any idea who's blackmailing you? Any chance of reconciliation with Barbara?"

"I have my suspicions, but it could be a number of people. As for Barbara, I'm not sure. She knows something's up, especially when she tried to withdraw money from our emptied account. She's given me many chances to come clean and I haven't."

He leaned forward. "Space is my only chance, until I get it all sorted out."

"Did you own up to your affair?"

He lowered his head. "I couldn't bring myself to do it. At this point I'm not sure it would help or not. You know she's barren, right?"

I nodded.

"How can I tell her I got another woman pregnant? It would destroy her."

"And letting her find out from a PI is better?"

We both leaned back in our chairs. I folded my hands behind my head searching for something meaningful to say. He remained quiet while tapping his fingers in rhythm on the chair's leather armrests.

"Do you need space to clear your head and take care of this?"

"No, Rich. I need to work. I need to make as much money as I can right now."

"We'll get started on Jenkins in the morning. Lou has my laptop."

"Lou?"

"Be here at nine o'clock tomorrow and we'll get moving."

"Will do. Thanks for hearing me out and not crucifying me. I apologize about the stress I caused."

I lifted my hand waving off his apologies.

"You can count on me from here on."

"Good, then you're my date tonight."

"Excuse me?"

"We're going to have a grand time at Pines's fund raiser this evening. You'll be taking Rosa's place."

"Do I have to wear a dress?"

It's nice to hear his sarcasm again.

"I'd prefer we go incognito. A tuxedo will do. I'll pick you up around 7:45."

"At my sisters; do you remember where she lives?"

"We'll find it. I'll escort you down to the lobby. Can I buy you a drink?"

"No thanks, I've got a few things to take care of."

We entered the VIP elevator, strapped ourselves in and let the free fall begin.

"You sure about the beer?"

"I better not."

"Suit yourself. See you in the morning."

As I walked toward the bar my cell buzzed. I froze when "restricted" popped up. I waved for Ty to come back.

"Hold on a second," I told him pointing to my phone.

"Rich Green here."

"Hi Rich, this is Sharon Smith."

I don't know a Sharon Smith, but she sounded polite so I asked, "Hi Sharon, how can I help you?"

"Are you free Monday at 10?"

"Depends on who you are and what it's about?"

"Didn't Sarah Givens tell you I'd be calling? I'm your producer."

I whispered, "It's okay" to Ty waving him off.

"I'm so sorry, she did tell me you'd be calling. Yes, 10 on Monday works for me. At the studio?"

"Yes, I'll see you then. I love doing new shows. They're so exciting. Ciao!" She hung up.

Thursday, August 25, 2010 8:00 PM
Robert Pines For Governor Fund Raiser

Ty became my new date to the black tie event after Rosa cancelled, still fuming over our last ordeal at Luke's. I hoped tonight would allow us to reconcile. Instead I'll be spending the night with Ty watching him enjoy the perks only a $10,000 per plate donation could bring.

The hostess greeted us with her perfect smile. She handed us our name badges and pointed to our table.

"Would you mind escorting us?" Ty asked her.

"I'll get someone over to help." She turned waving a waiter over.

"Don't start," I whispered to Ty. "Come on, Rosa." I grabbed his arm and pulled him into the grand ballroom.

"This place is amazing," Ty said."You been here before?"

"Many times. Pines holds most of his events here."

The Roseland Ballroom, located midtown, is one of the premier venues in New York City. The crystal plates, sterling silver dinnerware, and magnificent floral arrangements accented by the warm lighting create a spectacular ambiance. Hors de oeuvre's, mobile wet bars, and the friendliest staff of waiters bring it all together. There's no other venue which can transform such a meaningless gathering into a gala that'll be talked about for years.

My extreme generosity placed us at the number one table among the six other top donors. None of which I know, or even care to meet. We circled the unoccupied table and found our engraved brass nameplates standing in front of our dinner plate. I sat down. Ty fastened Rosa's badge on his left hand coat pocket. Then took off to grab a drink and mingle.

"Ty."

He turned back toward me.

"Bring me a beer," I said. Then lip synched, "And don't do anything stupid."

"Okay," he lip synched back.

The arrogance and stuffiness of these fund raisers drives me nuts. I could tell already this one promises to be no different. Gun controlists, environmentalists, atheists, and every other activist known to man will be in attendance. By the end of the evening, every one of them will have bent Pines' ear about their righteous ideals. I'll kick back, drink a few beers, and take it all in.

"Rich," a familiar voice shook me out of my trance. Pines emerged from the pack of boot lickers escorting him across the room. He grabbed a tall, stooped shouldered man by the elbow and headed my way.

"Rich Green. Chief Harry Moore. He heads up the Investor Protection Bureau. Someone you don't want to meet--if you know what I mean."

"Nice to meet you, Harry," I said displaying a fake smile. I tried to be discreet, but found myself giving him the once over. He's a perfect rendition of the prototypical government employee. Buzz cut on top, black frame glasses, sporting a thin mustache clipped at the ends of his mouth.

He hesitated before accepting my hand.

"Likewise, I'm sure."

His tuxedo clung to his awkward frame, some pieces too loose, while others fit too tight—a rental for sure. I pictured his normal dress consisting of a red paisley tie hanging too low, surrounded by a charcoal grey suit. I hate those guys.

"So," I said. "How long you been with the agency?"

"Five years or so," he replied. "How long you been wrecking companies?"

I leaned back in shock, "Excuse me?"

He walked away without responding.

"Always so pleasant?" I asked Pines.

"Don't mind him. He's having a tough day."

"I'll say."

I watched Moore grab a drink from the nearest mobile bar, down it, grab another, and head over to the tables. He walked around and took his seat--at my table. Great. This ought to be exciting.

"Excuse me, Bob. I need to go find my date before he gets himself in trouble."

He nodded before realizing what I'd said. "Did you say?" He pointed at me with a confused grin. "What did you just say?" His baffled look made me laugh.

"My assistant, Ty Gillian, stepped in for Rosa at the last minute. It's okay."

I waded through the sea of tuxedos and high-dollar sequined evening dresses searching for Ty. Knowing what I know about him, he'd be where the attractive, rich, and single women congregate--at the bar circling the dance floor.

On the way across the huge ballroom floor, I stopped to chat, hug, and shake hands of the few people I'd come to know over the years. Pines had managed to get himself caught in a debate between two investment bankers and two women. By the time I entered the circle, Moore emerged out of nowhere.

"Bob," he said. "If you'd increase the taxes on all these mergers we'd have less corruption. All you guys think about is making millions while the rest of us fund your lifestyle," he said pointing at the two bankers.

"What do you think Rich?" Pines asked me.

"Yeah, Rich, what do you think? This ought to be good, huh Bob?" Moore said nudging his superior with his elbow.

The whole group stood silent waiting on my response.

"I don't think higher taxes solve the problem. That'll dry up activity, costing the millions of you," I said pointing at Moore, "much more money. Instead of fighting the market, you should learn how to profit from it."

The group turned their eyes to Moore.

"Profit from it? How does anyone profit from greed and corruption?"

The eyes turned to me.

"You do everyday."

"How's that?"

All eyes on me.

"It keeps you employed," I said. "Without greed and corruption you wouldn't have a job."

Before he could counter, I tapped him on the shoulder. "I'll see at the table later. You look thirsty; I'll bring you a beer."

I walked off to the laughs in the background. Nothing like a righteous jerk to highlight a political fund raiser.

Monday, August 29, 2010 09:45 AM
FNN Studio

I arrived a few minutes ahead of schedule giving me time to settle down and prepare my mind. Opportunities like this don't come around often. I'd hate to blow it by rushing around unprepared. Warren Buffett doesn't even have his own show. My time has come!

"Rich, over here," a spunky, over-caffeinated young lady waved. She started over toward me, wearing a tight black dress hugging every inch of her pencil thin body. The heels of her knee-high leather boots clicked with each step she took. Her long, dark black hair hung past her shoulders with her bangs clipped even along her eyes. She resembled a modern day Cleopatra.

"Sharon?"

"Yes, pleasure to meet you," she said shaking my hand. "You'd think as often as you'd appeared on Sarah's program we'd have already met."

"You'd think."

"So, you ready to discuss some ideas and put this baby on the air."

"Yep." Either she's super excited or high-strung; maybe both. She led me over to a table cut off from the rest of the room by wall dividers covered with frayed fabric covering.

"So here's the deal. We start with a half hour show airing in the evenings between 8 and 10 PM. You'll be covering recent merger activity, and putting your spin on whether they're good or not. You can talk about companies that may be prime candidates as well as invite guests to appear for five minute segments. With me so far?"

She nodded her head encouraging me to say yes, which I did.

"Good. We'll tape the first five shows and air them to check ratings. We'll make any necessary adjustments and tape five more. If they turn out well, we'll sign a one year contract, and you'll be a celebrity."

"Sounds good to me."

"Before we go to production, we have to agree to the initial terms and disclosures."

She pulled out two stacks of forms. Each printed on legal size paper and well over an inch think.

"Don't worry," she said in her enthusiastic voice. "I'll explain the main points, and skip the legalese. You know how the lawyers are."

"Yes I do."

She cleared a spot on the cluttered table big enough to lay the paperwork, and sat down on one of the folding chairs. She pulled a pen from behind her ear.

"First disclosure. You can't talk about any stock you own, or thinking of buying and selling, unless you disclose your position during or beforehand. We're required to put the disclaimer on the screen, and you'll have to say it as well. Sign here on both copies." She pointed to the line. "And initial all the legalese on both copies on each packet."

After thumbing through 20 or so pages she grabbed the next packet.

"Second, our background check form. Even though we know you, we still have to run a background check. We don't need any surprises creeping up on us. You know what I mean?"

She pointed to the signature line and had me initial each page. When we got to the last page she asked, "If there's anything in your background that will come up, please note it right there. If not, write N/A and initial the box right there."

I initialed both copies without hesitation. She grabbed the last packet.

"You'll of course get one set of these for your records. The last packet contains your non-compete and compensation agreement. By signing this, you agree not to appear on any other program or network without advance written approval from your producer--me." She smiled. "Same drill, initial each page and sign the last one."

We finished and she grabbed the compensation packet, which I'm most interested in.

"We'll pay you $1,000.00 per episode for the first 10. If it's decided to extend the show, we'll negotiate the compensation then. Also, this gives FNN the right to cancel the show at anytime without reason. It also covers residuals if the show becomes syndicated or reruns pop up. It's our standard agreement. Initial each page and sign the last one."

I picked up the last packet thumbing through the pages again.

"There's quite a bit to read here, Sharon. Do I have time to review them first?"

"We're scheduled to shoot in three weeks. How long do you need?"

"A few days. I'd feel much more comfortable having my lawyer review. Just to make sure this doesn't hinder my operations. You understand, don't you?"

She put the pen on one of the packets letting out a sigh as she folded her arms.

"Can you have it back to me by Thursday morning?"

"Sure, I'll bring them here so we can discuss any changes."

She leaned back her arms still crossed over her midsection.

"I'll tell you now, we won't be making any changes. It's a take it or leave it deal. If we decide to extend the show, then we'll negotiate."

She put on her serious face, letting me know to move on.

"I got it. How should I get in touch with you?"

"Here's my card. Call me with any questions. Thanks for coming by."

"Thank you. I'll see you Thursday morning."

"Super! Look forward to it. Ciao!"

She stood up, shook my hand, and few out of the cubicle leaving both stacks of legalese behind.

On the way out I called Stephens.

"How's the celebrity?" He laughed in his own unique style then started choking.

"You uptown or at the dump?"

"Neither, why?"

"I have a wad of papers for you to review before I become a celebrity."

"When do you need them?"

"I need to bring them back by Thursday morning, and you can't change anything. It's a take it or leave it deal, I'm told."

"Non-competes and what-not?"

"Yep, all the boring stuff keeping you employed."

"It shouldn't take long. I can do it once I get back."

"From where?"

"I'm on the Island and won't be back until tomorrow. Had a wild weekend with some close friends. If you know what I mean?"

I know all to well what he means.

"I'll tell you about it next time we talk."

"That's okay, save the details. I'll send the forms by courier to the dump."

"You're coming with me next time Rich. I promise you'll be enlightened."

"I'll pass, I have plenty of light in my life already."

"You need to meet the Romano sisters, Rich, They're a hoot!"

"I'm sure. Hey, before I go, what's the status on Jenkins?"

"We'll be closing this week, so I celebrated early." He started his laugh, choke, laugh routine.

"I gotta go," I said and hung up.

Thursday, September 1, 2010 9:45 AM
Pine Street

Ty and I sat in my office as I explained the background on Chico. Since our talk he's become almost normal again. I'm still concerned about his future though. I hope he pulls it together.

The phone rang, "What's up Mark?" I said. "Before you answer, keep it business. No more talk about last weekend."

"You need to live a little Rich."

"What do you want Mark."

"I've wonderful news for you today. First, the FNN papers pose no threat. More important, we close Jenkins on Thursday--it's a done deal. This weekend paid off!"

I dismissed the last comment about the weekend. I'll dig into it deeper next time we talk. I hung up.

"We got it, they're ours!" I said.

"Who?" Ty asked.

"Jenkins and Jenkins. Stephens just wrapped them up."

"Awesome. When do we close?"

"Monday morning. We should be funded and headed to the bank by noon. In 90 days we'll start splitting the company and selling the pieces."

"How much did we make in the meantime?"

"We're selling Kemp's stock now, which will net about $750,000. We'll disburse the proceeds as per our agreement. You should take in around $125,000."

"When will you disburse it? I could use it asap."

"When's your next payment due?"

Ty smiled and said, "You can be a real jerk at times, but since you make me lots of money I forgive you. I have one last payment and I'll be making that one in person."

"I'll wire an advance of 50K and the rest will be paid once the funds clear."

"Perfect, thanks."

He left, and I called Reef.

"Keep an eye on Ty for the next few days. He plans on paying a personal visit to his blackmailer to make the last payment, whatever that means."

"I'll take care of it myself. While I've got you, we haven't come up with much on Mr. X. He either dodged us or he's still holed up in the apartment. I'm leaning toward the first option."

"I'm more concerned with Ty at the moment. We just closed Jenkins so Mr. X will probably make contact soon. Your portion will be disbursed next Friday."

"Great! I love working with you. I make lots of cash, and there's never a dull moment. I'll check back with you after awhile."

I hung up and called Stephens. Before he had a chance to talk I started my questioning.

"What did you mean about the weekend paying off?"

"Nothing. I entertained Kemp and some others at the beach house. Why?"

"Anything I need to know about?"

"There's a lot you need to know about. Where do I start?" Before he could continue his sinister laugh routine I cut in.

"Let me rephrase. I don't care about the escapades between you and the midgets, or the Parmesano sisters. Keeping this legit; that's all I care about. We're already treading thin ice; I don't need some embarrassing story showing up on the tabloids."

"Just grown men having fun, Rich. What's wrong with that?"

"Nothing--except he's married and you're buying his company using delicate inside information. We're cashing out stock he obtained using an alias. Just some minor technicalities. Nothing to bad."

"It's all good. He signed the papers Friday morning. I picked him up at noon. I got it covered. Enjoy the conquest and relax."

"What's with...never mind. We'll talk later. Thanks for the good news."

"One last thing. It's Romano, not Parmesano, and you need to meet them."

"Whatever," I hung up.

Mark and Ty each have great potential, but cut themselves short by living messed up lives. Either one can crash and burn at anytime--spelling trouble for all of us.

Friday, September 2, 2010 1:00 PM
Midtown

Reef didn't let Ty stray too far from sight. After stopping at his bank, he made his way across town, switching cabs a few times in an attempt to hide his tracks, but those rookie tricks don't work.

Reef has his own tricks. He uses three cars to follow his targets, when one pulls off another joins and so on. During his rotation, Ty had the cab pull over at the corner and he walked the rest of the way. Right into the same building Mr. X holed up in. He grabbed his phone.

"Rich, call me back asap!"

He parked across the street and down a few yards from the entrance so he could keep the entry doors in sight. He told the other two cars to park at each end of the street to watch for Ty. This building had no back entrance.

He sat there for about five minutes before his phone buzzed.

"Rich, you're not going to believe this." His adrenaline made him feel short of breath. "Ty just entered the same building we followed Mr. X to last week."

"What? Are you serious?"

"Yes, I'm serious."

"You don't think he's working both of us do you?"

"I don't know what he's doing yet, but we'll get to the bottom of it."

"Well, if you see anything else call me."

"I will," he said, about to disconnect when he heard sirens approaching and saw Ty exit the building. "Hold on Rich, Ty just left the building and he's in a hurry."

As Reef pulled away from the curb, three cop cars came flying down the road and stopped in front of the building. They pulled out their weapons and ran inside.

Reef sent his men a message to wait and observe. He followed Ty.

By now Ty graduated from a fast walk to a jog. Reef kept 10 yards or so behind him. He heard more sirens getting louder. Someone must have spotted Ty leaving and alerted the police. He tried to catch up to him, but before he could, a taxi pulled up and Ty jumped in. The police sped around the cab and kept going.

"Rasta? What the heck?" Reef said out loud. He hit redial.

"Rich, does Ty use your cabbie?"

"No, they don't know each other, why?"

"You sitting down?"

"Should I be?"

Reef replayed the entire ordeal to Rich as he maintained his distance on Rasta's cab. His men would find out what happened soon enough.

"Should I call Ty?" I asked.

"Call Rasta," Reef replied. "Ask him to come get you. See what he says. In the meantime I'll stay on him and see what my guys found out."

Rich did as instructed and texted, "call me" to Ty.

"I just texted him. What are they doing now?"

"Driving along 55th street. I'm a few car lengths behind them."

"Hold on, Reef. Rasta's on the other line."

"Hey Boss Man, what's going on? Do you need me today?"

"Yes, right away. When can you be at my apartment, it's of extreme importance."

After a brief pause, he answered. "I'm not even in the city Boss Man. It'll be a few hours at least. I text you when I get close."

"Don't worry about it, I'll drive myself. I'll catch up with you later."

"Sorry Boss Man..." I hung up before he finished.

"Reef, still there?"

"Yes, what'd he say?"

"He's not in the city, and can't be here for a few hours. They're up to no good."

"Hold on a second."

Reef pulled to the curb allowing the police cars to speed past. Rasta's cab took a left at the light ahead. The police cars didn't follow, but went straight through. By the time Reef could merge into traffic he lost the cab. He activated the push to talk feature on his cell.

"I lost the cab. Any of you in the area? Come back."

"Negative Reef, I stayed behind to see what happened," one replied.

"Negative again, I'm stuck on 57th. The cops surrounded the place quickly, and sealed off the roads."

"The cab looks like a Jamaican flag, make some calls to see if we can get some help," Reef replied.

Reef cruised the streets turning left than right every two blocks hoping to catch a glimpse of the cab. It would take a miracle in this city, but Reef and miracles have a past. He hit redial.

"Yeah, Reef," Rich said. "What do you have?"

"Nothing. I lost them."

"Any chance you'll find them?"

"They could be miles away or one block over. The longer it goes the less chance I have."

"I wouldn't waste any more time on it. I'm sure we'll hear from them soon."

Friday, September 2, 2010 5:00 PM
Rectore Street

I spent the last few hours contemplating my future. Even though I love the thrill of buying a company, it's becoming too much to handle. Looking out over the river from my balcony used to remove my stress, but not any longer. A permanent vacation from business may be in my future, my near future. I walked back to my kitchen to grab a beer as my cell buzzed.

"What's up Reef?

"Have you watched the news this afternoon?"

I plopped down onto the couch and reached for the stereo remote. I need mood altering music.

"No, I'm trying to relax. Why?"

"They found Jack Harvey, dead in his apartment."

I jumped up from the couch.

"Jack's dead? You sure?"

"It's all over the news."

I gulped down half my beer in one swallow.

"How'd he die?"

"He got stabbed in his apartment. The same apartment building Ty went in today. It looks like our boy Ty may be involved."

"Ty? No way."

I finished the rest of the beer.

"It also looks like your buddy Jack is. or should I say, was associated with Mr. X. And he's also, or again was, Ty's blackmailer."

It took a few seconds for this to resonate through my mind.

"Jack and Mr. X working together? And Ty killed him because of blackmail? No way, he's not capable."

"You never know what a man will do when pushed up against a wall, Rich. He came out of the apartment building minutes after Harvey's murder. It doesn't look good."

"Any witnesses? Did anybody see him?"

"I did! The cops swarmed the building looking for clues and evidence. There's a good chance both of your names will come up, especially if Harvey wasn't diligent in cleaning up his files."

"What a nightmare."

"You and Jack do any business together?"

"No, but Jack calls me all the time looking to join up with us."

"I need to ask you a question, Rich."

"Go ahead."

"Do you know anything about this?"

"Of course not Reef! How can you even ask that?"

"Sorry, but you and Ty have possible motives. Let's pray the connection between Jack and his friend Mr. X never surfaces."

Pray?

"Have you made contact with Ty or Rasta yet," Reef asked.

"Neither has returned a call."

"I'm going to look around Harvey's place if I can. Maybe I can get an idea of what's going on. We'll talk later." End call.

Instead of calling Ty, I sent a text to Rasta, ""Whvr u r and whtvrr ur doing, stop and bring Ty 2 my apt. I know he's with you."

I can't believe this. Jack working with Mr. X. Jack blackmailing Ty. Ty murders Jack. My dream of a long relaxing weekend slipped away.

CHAPTER TWO

Wednesday, September 7, 2011 3:45 PM

Chief Investigator Harry Moore stood behind the lectern. In less than ten minutes his elite group of agents will stretch the tiny room beyond capacity.

In the past, this room resembled most old government offices. Thick, cheap white tile with black specks formed the foundation. The grout, long since replaced by dirt and dust accumulated over the years. A few of the overhead fluorescent lights flickered, creating a dizzying strobe effect. The ceiling tiles without watermarks bore old cigarette smoke stains from years ago. Yellowed posters and faded sticky notes covered most of the gloomy eggshell white walls. The folding chairs with worn or missing cushions provided minimal relief to the backsides of the agents.

The remodeled room confirms the agency's transformation from ancient to high tech under Moore's tutelage. The out-dated overhead projector surrendered itself to the most up-to-date audiovisual apparatus available. Each desk comes equipped with laptop computers connected to the ceiling mounted HD projector and premium sound system. The cheap floor tile was replaced by soft grey carpet. The walls consist of insulated fabric panels holding prints and motivational posters.

All printed bulletins and memos gave way to emails and instant messages. The day of the inter-office envelope system no longer exists. Halogen bulbs, set in recessed pots, illuminate the room. Ergonomic chairs designed for comfort perform their job well, sometime's too well.

Today the high-tech room plays the perfect host to announce the next step in Moore's climb to the top. Once Robert Pines, current Attorney General became Governor of New York, Moore's rise to AG will be imminent. Nothing or nobody can stand between him and his destiny. It's so close he can taste it.

His long-standing relationship with Pines began in high school. They met at a Young Republicans fundraiser and stayed connected ever since. They both attended Columbia University and started their law careers at the same firm. Their long history together produced the basis of Moore's meteoric rise from field agent to Chief of The Investor Protection Bureau in five short years. Major headlines and personal loyalties grease the path for fast promotions. Moore mastered both. He had two years on Pines, but always played a subordinate role in their relationship. This will all change soon. Attorney General marks the beginning of his journey.

"Everybody grab a chair and be seated, we're about to begin," Moore said. The last of the stragglers came in and sat toward the back or stood along the walls. He had a packed house.

"I have several announcements this morning. If you've read your memos, you know agent Hope Brennan left the agency. She defected to the dark side. Instead of prosecuting the crooks who deceive and steal, she's decided to defend them. It would not be a good career move to associate with her. I suggest you cut all ties."

He focused his piercing stare toward one agent in particular.

"She's now the enemy."

The agents began whispering to each other. Before he lost control of the room, he motioned for them to be quiet.

"Again, don't be seen with her." He had a point to make.

Hope Brennan possessed deep-rooted Christian values and an unwavering thirst for ethical behavior. She worked hard to gain the respect of her peers throughout the agency, but created enormous dissension by refusing to break even the smallest of rules. She and Chief Moore did not get along well because of this. She modeled everything he despised.

"What I'm about to say must not leave this room. Does everyone understand?"

A few agents nodded, most did nothing.

"I asked," he paused for maximum effect. "Does everyone understand?"

This time they all nodded.

"Our esteemed AG, Robert Pines, will announce his nomination for Governor of this great state in three weeks. This means you can't discuss it for the next three weeks."

He noticed scattered eyes among the agents. Scattered eyes meant scattered thoughts and lack of focus. So he repeated, "Eyes off the laptops and look up here. Everyone got it? Nod your head for yes... Having Robert as Governor would be great for New York, and for our agency. All of us need to do our part to make this a reality. There's no better way to assure his victory than bringing a high profile case to trial. And winning it"

The agency's failure to prosecute the last two high profile cases became a problem for Chief Moore. Criticism from the press, and heavy pressure from Albany started to mount. The agency blew the first case because of a minor technicality due to an illegal search.

He blamed the second blown case on Brennan. She refused to testify against the defendant because of tainted evidence. Both of these cases damaged Moore's credibility and leadership. He can't afford another setback. He needs a big break to reestablish himself as front-runner to replace Pines as Attorney General. Whatever the cost, he will succeed.

The small talk and chatter in the room grew into an all out crescendo before the Chief took control.

"Settle down, we're almost done. All of you not working on a major case will be put on a new team. Reggie will email the new team roster this afternoon. Each team will meet with Reggie at the scheduled time to receive details on your new assignments. Those not on the roster will receive a separate email to meet in my office at 1630 today. Any questions before we leave?"

"Good," he continued. "One last thing. We need volunteers to work on the campaign. If you're interested see Reggie. He'll get you fixed up. Now let's get out there and bring those crooks to justice."

Thursday, September 8, 2010 11:45 AM
Chief Moore's office

"I'm calling it Operation Geronimo," Chief Moore said. "This will be huge if we pull it off."

With Attorney General Pines' pending entrance into the heated race for Governor, the Chief must capitalize on this opportunity. Opening a major case days before his announcement provides the momentum needed to win the nomination. Obtaining a guilty verdict before the election provides the catalyst needed for victory. More importantly, it will propel him into the vacancy he desires. There's no room for failure.

"As the packets indicate, I've worked on this sting for over a year. Recent activity has forced me to move quicker than I'd planned. I hand-picked you two to help me finish the case."

He looked each one in the eye.

"You've shown your loyalty and willingness to make things happen. I expect no less on this case, understood?"

Agents Joe Steele and Cody Hawkins nodded their heads. Both well versed in Moore's methods and philosophy of "all's fair" when it comes to justice.

Steele's lineage in law enforcement runs four generations deep. From brutality charges to concealing evidence, they've all spent time with Internal Affairs. He and Moore met four years ago while working on the Seth Burns case. Steele provided the agency with sensitive evidence securing the guilty verdict, Moore's biggest victory so far. He recognized Steele's generosity by appointing him Lead Investigator, with the agency. A decision he's come to regret.

"The public pays us to do a job," Moore continued. "They don't care about the details, they just want protection, and that's what we provide." He handed each their dossier. "It contains everything you need to get moving."

Cody Hawkins is the polar opposite of Steele--especially on the outside. Well groomed and always in the latest fashion, straight out of CSI. Inside, he's similar to Steele. He's vicious and relentless on the job. He'll do whatever it takes to win, provided his morals aren't compromised. He's the Chief's right hand man in waiting.

Moore handed each of them a sealed, legal sized envelope with "confidential" stamped across the front, and said, "You will not discuss this case with anyone but me. Not even with each other, understood?"

They both nodded again.

"Each of us has a separate, but connected role in this," he continued. "Take the files and go somewhere private to review them in their entirety. Do not deviate from the instructions set forth. We must keep this top secret until we make our move. Any questions before you're dismissed?"

They shook their heads, grabbed their folders, and headed out.

"Be here at 0900 tomorrow for our final briefing. Enjoy your reading."

Chief Moore kicked back in his chair and swung his feet up onto his desk. He retrieved a fine Cuban from the inside pocket of his coat, clipped off the end, and rolled it on his tongue, getting it wet and juicy. He savored the taste of fine cigars. His pre-victory celebration has begun. By this time next week Operation Geronimo will be in full swing.

Friday, September 9, 2010 9:00 AM
Chief Moore's Office

"I trust you two reviewed the dossiers," Moore asked. "You understand who we're dealing with?"

"For the most part," Hawkins answered. "Have a few questions though."

Moore pointed at Steele, "You?"

"One or two."

"Good. I hoped you would," Moore said as he handed each of them another sealed packet. "Your specific instructions. Don't open them until you receive the code word, Geronimo, texted to your phone. From that point, you'll have 30 minutes to read the envelope and take action."

He felt the excitement circulate throughout his body. This will be huge for the agency, for Pines, and of course himself. His plan has come to fruition. And better than he'd imagined.

"Questions?" Moore looked toward Steele.

"What if we're involved in something big when you text us?"

Moore's eyes burned a hole into Steele's. "Then drop it and proceed as instructed." He shook his head and raised his hands in disbelief. "Did you miss the part when I explained the importance of this mission?"

Steele squirmed in his chair.

"Hawk?"

"No, Chief. I'm good."

Steele kept his head pointed toward Moore, but slid his eyes toward Hawkins mumbling something profane under his breath.

"If you have something to say, let's hear it."

Steele waved his hand at Hawkins, "Shhh, he ain't worth it."

"What's up your butt, Steele? If you've got something to say to me, man up or shut up."

"Believe me, suck-up. I've got plenty to say," Steele stood up. "We can take this..."

"Sit down, jerk," Hawkins said. "You're nothing but a worn out ex-cop, Joe. You'll get your chance at me, but you'll reg..."

"Shut up--both of you. You can take each other out to the wood-shed after we bust these guys, but for now you'd better work together or I'll kick both your asses. Got it?"

They both looked in every direction, except straight ahead.

"This means yes," Moore said using an exaggerated nodding of his head.

"From here on, we'll have no communication with each other until my text. Memorize and destroy everything except the envelopes I just handed you. Destroy those immediately after you read them. We can't afford to jeopardize this by leaving crap behind. With me?"

"Yep," Hawkins answered turning toward Steele.

"What if we do think of a question?" Steele asked.

"There won't be any," Moore said clenching down on his teeth. "You'll understand once you read it."

"Let's do it," Hawkins said. "Until we meet again..."

Once Hawkins left, Steele got up and closed the door.

"Do you think we can trust him?"

"What's with you, Steele? Why do you constantly think everyone's up to something?"

"You know he and Brennan . . .?"

"Yes, I know. What does that have to do with anything?"

"Just that, he seems soft. This case requires muscle and skill. And I don't..."

"Think he has it?" Moore finished his sentence. "Look, Joe, not everybody handles things like you. Some of us use our heads first, and our fists last. Relax, you're on the same team."

"Sometime's I wonder. Like you said. we can't afford any mistakes."

Steele thinks everyone's crooked or hiding something. I call him paranoid he calls it carefu. Either way it gets old. When it comes down, and it will, my money's on Hawkins.

"Concentrate on your assignment. That's all you need to worry about. Now if you don't mind, I have other business to take care of."

Steele grabbed a magazine off Moore's desk and remained seated.

Moore snatched it from him, "Close my door on your way out."

Friday, September 9, 2010 2:15 PM
Hudson River Esplanade

Walking the Hudson River Esplanade ranks as one of my favorite activities. The esplanade became part of the Hudson River Park reconstruction project in 2003. Spanning five miles from Battery Park north bound past the Holland Tunnel, it's loaded with multiple playgrounds, ball fields, and resurrected piers; bringing millions of visitors each year.

These improvements cost New York a fortune, but brought about a two-fold benefit: renewed interests in the area by businesses, which increased property values significantly, plus, most of the renovations are free to enjoy.

I acquired my apartment during reconstruction. The hassle of dealing with the workers and the noise had its moments, but the end result proved worthwhile. Some of my best memories took place sitting on a bench, watching the world go by.

A high sun spreading its warmth, birds singing, and the light northern breeze, made it a perfect day to walk. The Hudson maintained its typical heavy traffic of boats and ships, but the boardwalk doesn't get real crowded during the weekdays. At times it's so congested you can't even walk, but today it's perfect.

My route for the day starts by walking south toward Battery Park. Then I'll circle back north to the tunnel and back again ending in front of my apartment. This five mile walk covers the entire length of the esplanade. I find it a great way to purge my mind often allowing me to take a fresh approach to life.

About two hundred yards into it my cell chirped.

"Hey Reef, what's up?"

"Have you heard from your boy, Ty, yet?"

"No, why?"

"We're at a dead end, We can't find him, Rasta, or the cab."

"They'll turn up."

"You don't understand, Rich. They just disappeared without a trace?"

I know where he's going with this.

"I'm starting to think they planned this whole thing out. It's hard to believe they could do something this sinister, but they're gone."

"That thought had crossed my mind. I just can't see Ty killing anyone; doesn't make sense. And Rasta? Why in the world would he get involved? He's a cab driver for crying out loud."

"I've seen people get knocked off for much less than Ty paid Harvey."

I walked toward the railing where a vacant bench awaited me. What Reef's saying does make sense.

"Then, maybe, he offered to pay Rasta the final payment in exchange for the ride?"

"If so, why would Rasta use his cab? It's not hard to identify."

"This is New York, Rich. Millions of people and thousands of cabs. Who pays attention to what cabs look like anymore? Plus, Ty didn't expect me to be there to see the whole thing play out."

"He knew about you tailing him."

"He tried losing me by switching cabs three times on the way over there."

"What does that prove?"

"Look, Rich. All I'm saying, he had motive, and I saw him flee the crime scene right about the same time the M.E. says Harvey died."

"How long have you known that?"

"Ten seconds before I called."

I got up from the bench, another weekend about to be ruined.

"Rich, you there?"

"Yeah, just thinking."

"Remember, God works in mysterious ways."

"If you say so."

"Something positive will come out of this, it happens all the time."

I continued my walk southbound toward Battery Park, blowing off the God comments. "Call me if you hear anything else. I appreciate you and your effort so far."

"I got your back. Relax, and enjoy the weekend. You deserve it." End call.

As I strolled toward the park, I noticed fathers, mothers, brothers, and sisters enjoying each other's company. I took a seat on a shaded bench across from one of the fields and watched as they played. Watching them calmed my anxious spirit. Maybe it's time to settle down and start a family. Rosa's ready, our finances look great, and I can work from home if I get bored.

I made the call.

CHAPTER THREE

Monday, September 12, 2010 4:10 PM
Pine Street

"Dude, where are you!" I yelled into the phone. "Rosa's waiting on us."

"Traffic, it's a mess out here today. I'll be there as quick as I can."

Why today? Of all the days I need to be on time, my new driver chooses to be late, why today! I sat down on one of the burgundy leather couches by the doors leading to Pine Street rehearsing my speech to Rosa. I had it down pat. Soon Rosa Milano-Green and I will be enjoying each other forever. She's going to make the perfect mother. Our life together will be sweet.

"Hey baby," I said. "We're running late. Sorry, I'll make it up to you."

"Okay. I'll be waiting, love you."

"Love you too."

The air-tight construction of my building provides shelter from the noise pollution New York made famous. Outside the doors, you experience the sirens, cars, taxi drivers laying on their horns, and all the other sounds big cities create in full surround sound. Inside, peace and quiet reign, until my driver runs late.

I reached over the arm rest finding the lever and reclined my seat. Ty's disappearance still lingered in my thoughts. Still no contact, though, from him or Rasta.

I dialed Rasta again, and again no answer.

I hung up and dialed Reef. It went to voicemail. I left a short message to call me. Next up, Stephens, and he answered.

"Who's party are you at?" The music in the background blasted through the earpiece. "The Limburger sisters?"

"You're a funny guy, Rich," he screamed trying to overtake the music. "No. Just hanging with some close friends, about ten of them." He started his laugh, cough, choke routine.

"Have you heard from Ty?" I tried talking over the deafening DJ's selection.

"What? I can't hear you."

Through the window I saw three squad cars pull up to the curb.

"Forget it." I hung up switching my attention to the activity outside.

Two goons emerged from the first car. Each wearing dark suits, crew cuts, aviator sun glasses, and the mandatory ear piece. The leader gave me a long stare-down and marched to the concierge desk. The uniforms got out and stationed themselves by the doors.

As my dad used to say, "someone's in a heap of trouble."

Monday, September 12, 2010 4:13 PM
Show Girls Lounge

Agent Hawkins pulled up in his government edition Crown Victoria, escorted by two unmarked Impala cruisers. His instructions were clear and precise. Be in position by 4:25 and wait for the Chief's text. If there's no text by 4:45, they're to abort the mission. If one of them failed to apprehend their targets at the appointed time, the entire operation could be compromised. He's determined not to be the one to blow the case.

Hawkins didn't mind tailing his perp to a strip club. He preferred the high-end establishments for his pleasure, but this makes a perfect setting for what's about to go down.

After directing the plain clothed officers around the perimeter, he entered the sleaze parlor, flashed his badge to the strung-out doorman, and raised his fingers to his lips to be quiet.

"I'm not here to cause you any problems," Hawkins whispered. "I need to see the manager right now. Where's he at?"

He was led through the narrow gap between the bar and the buffet table. The spotlights aimed at the stage cast the only light in the joint. For enough cash, the dancers left the well lit stage to perform private maneuvers in the dark. Hawkins caught a glimpse of his target waving Franklins at the ladies as he passed. He knows the drill.

The skinny, tattoo infested doorman stepped halfway into the manager's office. He jerked his head indicating he wasn't alone.

"What's up Bruce?" a rough voice escaped from the office.

"There's a cop here to see you," he said, and stepped aside.

Hawkins squeezed passed Bruce, brushing up against his greasy mullet as he entered the dimly lit room. The manager sported a goatee and bald head. He sat behind a small desk cluttered with ashtrays, empty beer bottles, and magazines. Autographed posters of famous porn stars covered the walls. The one lamp in the corner struggled to cut through the dense smoke filling the air.

With a cigarette hanging out of his mouth he asked, "What do you want?"

"One of your patrons will be escorted out of here," Hawkins stated. "I'll make it as painless as possible. You'll need to stop the show in about 20 minutes until we take care of business."

"It'll cost me too much money," he answered. "Show me who you want and I'll make sure he's alone."

They both stepped out of the office, and Hawkins pointed toward the stage.

"You see the short, fat man at the far edge of the stage? The one surrounded by three girls? That's him."

"It figures you'd pick one of my best customers."

"Maybe you'd be willing to arrange conjugal visits for him?" Hawkins laughed while the other two stood there. "It would keep your cash flow intact." They still didn't laugh.

The manager gave him the "don't you have business to take care of" look.

As Hawkins walked away he said, "I make my move in a few minutes. When I stand up and approach him, please clear the area."

On the way back, he stopped at the buffet table and fixed a plate of fried chicken and mashed potatoes. He sat three tables behind his target, took a few bites of his meal, and sent his text.

Monday, September 12, 2010 4:14 PM
Uptown

Agent Steele honed in on his target's cell phone GPS signal to an up-scale brownstone owned by Dr. Marvin Oliver, one of the most popular cosmetic surgeons in New York. His billboards and commercials were plastered everywhere. Although the target visits this house often, he doesn't come here for breast augmentation.

Steele directed his uniformed backups around the block to watch the rear of the house. How embarrassing it would be if he escaped through the back door. Once in place, they'd enter from the front and make the catch.

Steele stood at the curb a few houses down gauging the layout. He'd played this scenario several times in his mind. He wanted to make sure he didn't overlook any tiny detail.

He pulled the wire holding his microphone up close to his mouth and whispered, "Unit 1, you in place?"

"Roger, unit 1 in place."

"Excellent," he motioned to the two officers standing behind him to spread out.

"On my command we move," he said into the mic again.

"Copy, unit 1 ready."

Hawkins wolfed down the greasy chicken and waited for the signal. He tried to maintain focus on his subject, not the enticing action on the stage. Once he received the word, he'd alert his backup and the raid would begin.

For a low-end dive, the action appealed to Hawkins' lustful desires. He found one dancer in particular to be his kind of woman. She looked familiar, but then again they all did. He made a mental note to revisit on his own time.

The target continued flashing wads of cash toward the stage, but none of them gave him any notice. He looked toward the manager's office and nodded as if to say make your move.

The cell screen lit up. Time to move. "NOW"

He counted to five and stood up. Once his team entered he made his move.

"Mr. Stephens?" Hawkins asked.

"Yeah, what the hell do you want? Can't you see I'm busy," he replied. He continued waving his cash at the girls. "Get away from me, you pervert, I'm not into your kind of kinky crap."

"Mr. Stephens, we can do this the easy way or the hard way,"

"What are you talking about?" He lifted his hands in confusion, sticking the bills in Hawkins' face. "I told you get away from me, or I'll shove my fist right down your throat."

"You think?" Maybe that works on his women, but not a man of Hawkins' stature.

"Listen Pal, you'll find what you need at the gay place. It's two buildings down--on the right."

Hawkins waved his backup over.

"Agent Cody Hawkins," he said flashing his badge, "from the New York Attorney General's office, and you, hotshot, are under arrest. You can come peacefully or I'll drag you out of here kicking and screaming. What's your pleasure?"

He turned toward and pointed his finger at Hawkins, "Let me tell you..."

Before he could finish, they grabbed him, forced him down, and cuffed him.

"I gave you the choice," Hawkins said. He pointed to the door, "Get him out of here, It's time to go home."

"What about my money," Stephens yelled out. "My money's on the table, let me get it."

"How much?"

"Two grand!"

"You won't need it where you're going." On the way out he grabbed the DJ's microphone and said. "Dances on the house, two thousand dollars worth."

The manager flew from his office trying to beat the other patrons to Stephen's money.

"Do you work for Moore?" Stephens yelled, "because if you do, you're through."

"Save it for the judge," Hawkins told him.

As they left Hawkins sent his confirmation, "done"

Monday, September 12, 2010 4:40 PM
Uptown

Steele's cell screen illuminated. The time has come. He unsnapped his holster and removed his sidearm. Even though there's no chance his target will be packing, Steele loves the thrill of flashing his weapon. The one thing he misses from his days walking the beat.

He crossed the extra wide sidewalk and climbed the six stairs, two at a time, to the top of the stoop. He spanned the horizon and took a deep breath. One, two, three... he banged on the door.

"Who's there?" a soft female voice asked.

"Police, open up!" He loved saying this.

As the door started opening, Steele stepped back and unleashed a wicked front kick using his heel to blast the door open. The force propelled Mary Oliver backward landing on the stairwell behind her.

"What the heck!" Dr. Oliver yelled as Steele and his backups rushed through the door toward him.

"What's going on here?" he yelled again. "You just can't storm into someone's house without a warrant!"

As they swarmed the house, Steele said "Shut up. Where's he at?"

"Where's who?"

"Your wife's boyfriend, that's who."

"Look what you did to her," Oliver said leaning over her wiping the blood from her right cheek. "You better have a good explanation for this intrusion or I'll have all your badges."

Steele never acknowledged the comment.

"Up there," Steele pointed. Two of the cops climbed over the couple on the way up the stairs. Mary shrieked as one of the cops smashed her finger between his boot heel and the carpeted stair.

"There's nobody up there, and my wife doesn't have any boyfriend," the doctor stood up pointing his finger at Steele. "I suggest you leave now unless you have a warrant."

Steele pushed past the doctor making his way to the kitchen. He leaned tight against the door frame. In one smooth motion he grabbed his gun with both hands and swung into position facing the backdoor. The sinking feeling of failure crept into his mind.

"All clear up here," one of the cops yelled.

"Damn!" Steele yelled storming back to the stairwell.

He yanked open a door under the stairs—a closet. He pushed the coats aside. Nothing.

"You'd better exit my house now," Oliver said breathing heavily.

"Did I tell you to speak!" Steele pointed his gun at the couple.

She screamed, and the doctor pulled his wife closer.

"Put your gun away, there's nobody here other than us."

"Tell me where he's hiding...woman. Or I'll make your life a living hell."

Mary started balling, holding her hand tight to her chest. The tears mixing with her blood trickling from the gash below her cheek where the door smacked her earlier.

"Quit crying you baby. I'll be out of here once you give me his whereabouts."

"I know the chief of police, and he'll be hearing from me. You'd better believe that."

"How well do you know him?"

"We play golf together every other weekend."

"Well then, he can pay for your next round. She'll be fine. After all, you are a doctor, aren't you?"

They all laughed and left the house slamming the door behind them.

Steele sent, "Negative"

He blew it!

Monday, September 12, 2010 4:43 PM
Pine Street

I decided to wait outside for my driver. The cops standing around motionless gave me the creeps. As I approached the always turning, revolving door, one of the cops stepped in front of me. At about 6'5" tall and 250 pounds, I wouldn't be able to push him aside. I resorted to an old tactic--ask him to move.

"Excuse me officer, I'm waiting on my cab."

He didn't respond, but he didn't move either.

"Do you mind? I need to catch my cab."

He still didn't move. As I attempted to go around him a voice whispered in my ear.

"Mr. Green, put your hands behind your back. You're under arrest."

I recognized the voice and tried to turn around, but the cop blocking the door grabbed me by the shoulders and said, "I wouldn't do that. Now do as you're told and put your hands behind your back--Scuz Ball!"

"What's going on here? Nobody talks to me . . ."

Before I could finish, two of the cops wrestled me to the floor and pinned me face first on the tile. In seconds they had me cuffed and lifted back to my feet.

"Next time the Chief tells you something, you'd better do it--Scuz Ball!"

That's the voice all right, Chief Moore from Pines's fundraiser.

"So, Harry. This your way of getting back at me from the other night?"

"Call it what you'd like, Green. Keeping your mouth shut for once seems the best strategy."

"How 'bout I call my lawyer."

"No need," Moore replied. "You'll be seeing him soon enough."

"What does that mean?"

He proceeded to read me my rights and forced me out to the street. I hadn't noticed the crowd that gathered outside the building. The television, radio, and newspaper crews rushed us once we hit the sidewalk.

Amidst all the flashes and reporters throwing questions at me, I bowed my head trying to get to the squad car as fast as possible. However, the Chief held me by the cuffs while he took his sweet time answering as many questions as he could. All the while, the cameras broadcasted my face all over the country.

I kept my head down while he gloated over his "conquest." I wondered how foolish I looked in front of the world. Pulling away from Moore's grip, I lifted my shoulders, and looked into the cameras trying to appear calm and unashamed. Paybacks are hell.

Before he finished, he reached up for a high-five and said into the microphones, "Geronimo!"

Monday, September 12, 2010 5:30 PM
Luke's Lobster Financial District

Rosa sat by herself at Luke's. She left five messages for Rich, and even called Rasta, but neither of them answered. She finished her club soda and went to pay her tab.

Storr worked behind the counter again tonight. He remembered their last visit resulting in seafood, french fries, and broken plates all over the floor.

"You don't look real happy tonight," he said. "Can I get you something on the house?"

"No thanks, my husband, who says he's changed stood me up. He won't even answer his phone."

"I'm sorry to hear that. Maybe something happened and he's just running late."

"Or maybe he's just a selfish jerk after all. I should've known better."

Her phone buzzed and she grabbed it out of her purse. She wasn't sure if she wanted it to be Rich or not. It wasn't.

"Hello, Martha," Rosa said.

"Are you okay?"

"I think so. Why do you ask?"

"Is Rich with you?"

"No, he never made it over here. What's going on?" Rosa felt her anxiety increase with each passing second.

"Are you by a TV?"

Yes, why?"

"Just watch the news and then call me back!" she hung up. Rosa looked for the remote and didn't see it.

"Storr," she yelled. "Where's the remote, I need to watch FNN."

"Hey lady, the Giants' game's about to start. You can't change it." One of the patrons shouted back at her.

"Please just for a few minutes, please."

They mumbled something, and she grabbed the remote from Storr and changed the channel.

She saw Sarah Givens and Chief Investigator Harry Moore discussing "Operation Geronimo."

Rosa listened to the interview for a few minutes, wondering what this had to do with her and Rich. Maybe he's a special guest this evening? He would have called, unless he planned to surprise me.

The she saw it.

Up on the screen, big as life, Rich Green, handcuffed and escorted out of his office building. Reporters were shouting questions, and cameras flashing, just like a criminal getting arrested. And Rich with his head bowed down trying to avoid the cameras.

The next video showed a handcuffed man, Mark Stephens, pulled from a strip club by two officers. He fought like crazy until the officers subdued him.

Pictures of Ty Gillian came up next. The ticker asked viewers to call the agency if anyone spotted him.

The ticker then changed to a narrative, Richard Green, owner of Green Enterprises and one of FNN's regular guest hosts was arrested on several counts of insider trading and obstruction of justice. The result of a year long sting Chief Moore referred to as, "Operation Geronimo."

She hit recall on the remote, and redial on her phone. Martha answered on the first ring.

"I'm sorry, Rosa. I can only imagine how you must feel right now."

"For starters, I feel shocked, stunned, overwhelmed, and angry all at once. Can you imagine that? What should I do now?"

"We could start by praying for guidance and strength."

Here we go again with the God thing. I can always depend on Martha, but her insistence that God controls everything tends to get in the way of our friendship.

"Or, by getting a lawyer," Rosa said pacing back and forth across the restaurant. "I'm not sure prayer will help at this moment."

"It always helps, Rosa. How about I help you find a lawyer, while keeping you in my prayers?"

"That'll be great. I'd better get home before it gets much later. I have surgeries scheduled all day tomorrow."

"Call me when you get a chance. I'm here if you need me."

"I know you are Martha, and I appreciate it more than you know. I'll call you tomorrow. Thank you."

"No need for thanks, friends helping friends."

In the flash of an eye, Rosa's world became much more complicated. She rubbed her belly saying, "Don't worry honey. Your Father will be all right."

Monday, September 12, 2010 5:35 PM
Back of Squad Car

Getting carted around the city in the back seat isn't a new experience for me. Doing so with my hands cuffed to a railing breaks new ground. I can't recall ever sensing this type of humiliation and embarrassment. It's overwhelming.

"Excuse me, Harry. May I ask what's going on here?"

"Sure, but first let me remind you anything you say can and..."

"I know...will be used against me."

"Proceed at your own peril, Green."

"Why did you arrest me?"

"Because I can."

He smiled, trying to get me to say something damaging.

Instead, I said, "Okay. And..."

"We've watched your illegal activity over the last four years, and now we're ready to put you away for a long, long time."

"On what account? I've done nothing illegal."

"We'll let the court determine that."

He turned around and looked at me through the side view mirror. As he nodded his head, he said, "Yes Mr. Green, we shall let the court decide the fate of you and your cronies."

I leaned back, and thoughts of my past raced through my mind. Everything I ever did wrong came up. Does he know about Mr. X? About Sperry? What about my spot on FNN? I realized none of that mattered right now. The thought of Rosa sitting alone waiting for me ripped my heart out.

"Hey Harry, may I make a phone call?"

"Not until you are booked and processed, and you may address me as Chief."

"Okay, Chief. May I make a quick phone call to my wife? She's been waiting on me since 4:30."

I watched him crack a devious smile and knew his answer before he responded.

"Poor thing," he said. "I bet she s part of your scheme? Maybe we should go by and pick her up as well."

"She has nothing to do with my business. Leave her alone."

"What did you say her name is?"

"I didn't."

It's time to stay quiet until Stephens shows up.

Tuesday, September 13, 2010 9:35 AM
Dix Hills, NY

"Hi Hope, this is Martha Reynolds. Call me as soon as you can, I have a client for you. Bye, bye and God bless."

Martha's friendship with the Brennan's goes back to grade school. She remembers meeting Hope's mother, Samantha, in first grade at a field trip to the zoo. The shy Samantha sat alone on the bus, Martha, who never stopped talking, spotted her and grabbed the seat next to her. Samantha invited Martha to her church and soon led her to faith in Jesus.

Hope's father, Bill, and her brother were best friends. The four of them became inseparable. They attended church camps in the summer, and helped grow their youth ministry to well over 100 kids before heading their separate ways.

Somehow, through the grace of God, three of the four reunited in New York. Martha's brother never returned from Vietnam. They remained best of friends, until last year.

Three years ago Hope approached Martha with a moral dilemma concerning her faith and her job as investigator with the Investor Protection Bureau. After much prayer and tears, Martha encouraged Hope to follow God's path and break away from the agency.

This did not please Bill. He felt proud his daughter chose the agency over practicing law. Even though Hope tried to convince him she made the decision on her own, he didn't believe her. He put the blame on Martha. This drove a wedge in their relationship.

"Hi Hope," Martha answered her phone before the first ring ended. "Do you know my friend Rosa, the surgeon? I've had her over a few times."

"Her name doesn't ring a bell. Why?"

"Didn't you see the news last night about Rich Green's arrest?"

"Yes of course, Martha. I still keep tabs on those guys at the agency. Moore's a real winner. If you know what I mean?"

"I remember our talks about him, precisely why you should take the case."

"What case?"

"The Rich Green case."

"I don't understand?"

"He needs you your help."

"I don't even know him, plus I'm sure he already has a lawyer."

"They arrested his lawyer, and my friend Rosa is carrying his baby."

"I'll be there in an hour."

Martha called Rosa, and as expected, went straight to voicemail. "Rosa, this is Martha. I found you a lawyer!"

Tuesday, September 13, 2010 9:45 AM
Huntington Station, NY

Hope sat silent behind her desk for a few minutes. She bowed her head and prayed, "Dear Lord I know you put me here to do your will. If taking this case fits your plans, please give me a sign. Thank you Jesus for your mercy and grace. I ask of you to please protect Rosa and her unborn baby, and do your will with them. It's in your mighty name, Amen."

She grabbed her Bible and randomly opened to Proverbs 20. The two verses catching her eye were 18 and 24. "God does talk to us," she said aloud.

Verse 18 says, get good advice when you make your plans. Before you start a war, find good advisors. And verse 24 says, The LORD guides our steps, and we never know where he will lead us.

She scrolled her contacts and found the one she needed. It's been awhile since they spoke, but he's always there when she needs him.

"Well, well, well," he said with the sarcastic enthusiasm he's known for. "Ms. Hope Brennan, attorney-at-law. To what do I owe this unexpected pleasure?"

"I may be taking a huge case, and will need your help."

"How about, it's great to hear from you Stan! Or how is life after death?"

"You're right Stanley. It's great to hear your voice, and I'm sorry for not keeping in touch with you. Now can you meet me in 30 minutes at my parent's house?"

"I don't know Hope. I do have things going on you know. I am busy right now. And you can call me Stan. Stanley is soooo..."

"Nerdy?"

"Yes, and you're not off to a great start asking for my help."

"Oh stop! Must I beg you?"

"Yes, you must."

"All right. Please meet me at my parents house in 30 minutes, I beg of you. Please!!!! How's that?"

"Well. . ."

"Thanks," she said, and hung up before he could change his mind.

Hope set her call forwarding, grabbed her brief case, and headed out of the office. She'll meet up with Stanley to drive to Martha's together.

On the way, she realized the scope and magnitude of this case. It's a big-time opportunity. Is she ready for the headlines? Is she ready for the scrutiny? Her adrenaline started pumping. She'd finally get the chance to square off against the Chief. How sweet would victory taste after beating him!

"First things first," she said aloud. "Get yourself hired."

Tuesday, September 13, 2010 10:15 AM
Dix Hills, NY

Hope pulled up to Stanley's car and motioned for him to come with her. Martha lived five blocks away. She wanted him in her car so he couldn't get away. She'll need his expertise for sure.

Hope met him for the first time during a conference at the church he once pastored. Things didn't work out well for him, and he resigned under pressure from the elders. Even though he was exonerated of all wrong doings, he felt betrayed and lost his faith.

One day soon, I'll help him reunite with the Lord, was her hope.

He now makes his living helping others find the truth--whatever that is. He puts his military background in computer programming, explosive technology, and high-tech surveillance to good use. He's on the right team.

He jumped into Hope's car and she said, "Thanks for meeting me here Stanley, I mean Stan. It means a lot to me."

"No problem, but you owe me big," he replied giving her a cynical smile. "Lunch's on you today. And I'm starved."

"You're on!"

"So tell me, what are you working on that's so important?"

"Do you know who Rich Green is?"

"Is he a preacher or something?"

"Hardly," she replied laughing. "He's an investor. One of the big boys on the street. He buys and sells companies all over the world."

"And he's a Christian?"

"Not that I'm aware of."

He looked at her puzzled. "I thought you only helped Christians?"

"I do, but it's time to branch out a bit."

"Anyway, I've never heard of him, but that shouldn't surprise you since I keep all my money under my mattress."

"It doesn't surprise me at all. You're totally oblivious to the world around you."

"No, I'm just not falling for the media bull crap anymore. The trilateral commission owns everything and..."

"Anyway," she cut him off before his tirade got underway. "They arrested him last night along with his lawyer. Some guy named Ty is still on the loose."

"Why?"

"Insider trading violations and obstruction of justice, according to Chief Moore."

He shook his head a few times and pursed his lips together, before an inquiring smile formed.

"Let me see if I'm tracking with you. Does this have anything to do with settling a score with your former employer? A man named Harry Moore?"

"There's more to it than that. He needs my help and I need yours. There's no telling what Moore is capable of doing. He wants the Attorney General position badly. This could be the case that gives it to him."

"And you're going to thwart his evil, sinister plan. Did you ever consider the possibility Green is guilty as charged?"

"I don't have enough information to make that determination yet. That's why we're going to visit Martha."

"I'm tracking, but how does she fit in to the whole deal?"

"Her close friend Rosa and Rich are married... and she's looking for a lawyer to get Rich out."

As they pulled into the driveway of the well-maintained English Tudor, Stan said, "Let's check it out. I'm up for some excitement. After we eat, of course."

Hope smiled. "Of course. Let's pray before we go in."

"Go ahead, Hope. I'll meet you by the front door," he said and exited the car.

She prayed quickly, grabbed her stuff, and headed to the door. Stan had already entered the house by the time she got there, so she walked in without knocking.

"I see you two have already met," Hope said as she gave Martha a big loving hug.

"Thanks for coming by. I talked with Rosa a few minutes ago, and she'll be calling us in about 30 minutes. In the meantime I'll explain what's going on."

"Before we get started, do you have anything to munch on?" Stan asked. "Hope here pulled me away this morning before I had a chance to eat breakfast."

Martha looked at Hope.

"Don't mind him, he's always hungry," Hope said.

"Cookies, crackers, something to hold me over until she takes me to eat," Stan said. "I'll eat while you two discuss the case."

Martha looked at Hope again expecting an explanation. Hope shrugged her shoulders.

"There's crackers in the pantry over there," Martha pointed. "And soda in the fridge, help yourself."

"Thanks, I will," he said and headed to the kitchen.

"What's his deal?" Martha whispered once he slipped out of range.

"He's a genius with an insatiable appetite," she said. "Tell me what you know."

Martha explained what she knew about the case, which wasn't much. The one fact she did know, Richie's arraignment took place in three hours.

"Martha, give Rosa my cell number. Let her know I'll be there to help him post bail. We need to leave now or we'll miss it."

"Did you say we?" Stan shouted from the kitchen.

"Yes, grab a doggy bag and let's go," Hope answered. "We'll pick up your car later."

Tuesday, September 13, 2010 10:45 AM
Chief Moore's Office

Chief Moore sat behind his desk looking through the files of cases he'd assigned to his newer agents. He needed to discover a new talent. Someone he can develop into a crack agent; someone like himself.

Nothing fired him up more than blowing an easy assignment, especially by an agent with Steele's experience. It'll only be a matter of time before Steele would screw something else up. A loud knock on the door brought him back to reality.

"Who is it?" he shouted.

"Agent Steele. Can I come in?"

"Hold on a second," he yelled while he straightened up his desk. "Come in."

Steele rushed through the door and stood in front of Moore. "You'll never believe what happened?"

"What did you screw up this time?"

Steele glanced away from the Chief. unable to look him in eye after failing to obtain his target.

"Get on with it," Chief said. "Can't you see I'm busy?"

"Remember the murder from last week? The Jack Harvey character?"

Moore perked up when he heard Harvey's name.

"What do you know about it?"

"Check this out. One of my guys, Sonny, at the station told me an eye witness can put Ty Gillian at the scene of the crime. She recognized his picture from the news."

Hmm, this may be good. It ties up a few loose ends.

"She saw him get into a cab, said it looked like a Jamaican flag," Steele added.

"What'd you say?"

"The cab he got into looked like a Jamaican flag, why?"

"Call your guy right now and tell him don't go public with this info yet," Chief said standing up. "Get Reggie involved. Have him call Smitty, and tell him there's a pending investigation that will be compromised if this gets out. I need to see her right away. Did you get her name and address?"

"No, but I will."

The Chief grabbed his phone and headed out of the office. He turned back to Steele, who just stood there.

"Well, let's go!" he shouted at Steele. "Call Hawkins and tell him to meet me at Harvey's building. Text me her info. Get moving!"

On the way to his car, the Chief sent his own text, "what the hell were you doing there."

He ran to the parking garage and took off to his car. This may just blow up in my face.

***

Steele left the office and called Sonny. Once he got the details, he went to see Reggie as told. He sent the Chief her name and address. As far as calling Hawkins, screw that, this is my lead. He headed over the Harvey's building to meet the Chief.

***

The Chief's phone lit up, "Chief, Hawk cant be there, I'll meet u at 320 W 49th st."

"Great," Chief yelled out. "I need Hawkins for this."

He threw his phone down and made a classic movie style u-turn causing oncoming traffic to swerve and skid. The horns and gestures didn't faze him at all. He got back on track, and heard his phone ring, "What do you want now?"

After a brief silence, he heard a familiar voice respond. "Is that any way to talk to your superior?"

He looked at the screen and saw Robert Pines' name. He slammed on his brakes stopping inches before smashing into the car stopped in front of him.

"Sorry Bob, I thought you were one of my agents." Wrong thing to say.

"Is that how you talk to your agents, Harry?"

"Not usually Sir, but we just received some valuable information linking Ty Gillian with the murder of Jack Harvey, and we need to suppress it for the time being."

"The guy you failed to apprehend?"

"Yes, and I'm a little stressed about it at the moment."

"Me too, that's why I called," Pines said. Chief smiled and waited for the congratulations he expected.

"Are you out of your mind?" Pines yelled. "Are you trying to embarrass me and the entire agency?"

"I don't understand Bob. I was cnly..."

Pines cut him off in mid-sentence.

"The primaries are less than two months away, and you arrest one of my top contributors? The media and my opponents are going crazy saying this is politically motivated. I've dropped 10 points in two days. Plus, Green is a personal acquaintance. How could you do this without talking to me first? Be at your office in 20 minutes." He hung up.

Chief called him right back.

"Bob, I understand how you feel about this without having all the facts. Can we make our meeting in a few hours? I'll explain it all when I get there. I really need to interview this witness."

"Yes, you will explain all the facts when I see you in 20 minutes. Don't make me wait!" he hung up again.

Tuesday, September 13, 2010 11:05 AM
Chief Moore's Office

The Chief rushed back to his office and arrived with only seconds to spare. By the time he reached his office he was winded. Pines and his public relations specialist, Billy Williams, were waiting for him.

"Sorry to keep you waiting, I got here as soon as I could," Chief said. "Can I get you something to drink?"

"No. We're not here for drinks," Pines snapped back. "Tell me what in the world you're doing and why."

"About two years ago I received an anonymous tip about some insider trading going on at a company called

InCaHoots. We investigated them and found some irregularities, but not enough to be worthwhile. Do you remember?"

"Vaguely," Pines said.

"Well, about a year later we received another anonymous tip. We believe from the same guy, on a company called Diaboll, Inc. Once again we found some minor violations, but nothing we could make stick. Then last year the tip was on Sperry, Inc."

Chief looked at Pines. Pines looked back at him.

"What's all this have to do with Green?"

"I'm getting there. Two weeks ago we received information about CEO Steve Kemp from a company Green just bought called Jenkins and Jenkins. Apparently Mr. Kemp had been buying and selling shares under an alias. Green found out about it and didn't report the activity as he's required. He also used the information to blackmail Kemp into selling him the company at a discount."

"What else?"

"All four companies were purchased by Green and his team, using the inside information. It all came together so quickly, we had to act fast. I should have called you, but I thought it would be better if you didn't know about it, especially with the election coming up."

"And this murder? How does that fit in?"

"Jack Harvey provided the tips to Green. Jack wanted in on more of the action and threatened Green with going public if he refused. So Green had his accomplice Ty Gillian, take him out."

"I don't buy that for one second. I know those guys and there's no way they'd kill anybody. And I don't believe Green would be so stupid to use the information as you allege."

"Jack Harvey was also involved in an extortion scheme against Gillian concerning an affair and pregnant mistress. Gillian was seen by a credible eye witness standing over the dead body in Harvey's apartment, giving us an air-tight case. Motive and location!"

"This is too much," Pines said. He got up and paced back and forth across the office. "Bill, what can we do about this?"

"Well, Bob, we can play it as Moore acting on his own, without your approval, since you and Green are friends. He can take full responsibility and let you off the hook."

"I like it so far," Pines said.

Chief felt the beads of sweat forming at his hairline.

"I need some water," Chief said. "Do you guys need anything?"

Pines waved him off and he left the office. He checked his phone, but still no text, only a missed call from Steele, which he'd return later. He grabbed a bottle of water and went to the bathroom to wash his face and cool down.

When he returned to his office, Pines and Williams were seated again.

"Okay Harry, here's what we're going to do," Williams said. "You're going to go on the air, and publicly state that although you can't divulge the particulars of the case, one of your agents acted outside of Agency rules resulting in a reprimand, and Pines had no prior knowledge of the case."

"I'm not liking that too much," Chief replied. "We acted exactly like we should have. I think you should state that you understand how this looks being so close to a tight election, but duty called and you answered. You can also talk about your prior friendship with Green, but again duty called and you answered. You can pardon him after you win."

Pines looked confused about the direction he should take.

"Look at it this way, Bob," Chief added. "You're coming clean on all counts with my strategy. You didn't know, and you're standing on your morals. No questions left to answer. Billy's leaves a lot of unanswered questions, which is the last thing you need right now."

"I think he's right Billy," Pines said.

"I do need a favor to make this all come together, Bob," Chief asked. "Call Lieutenant Robert Smith and tell him not to release any information about the eye witness since it's part of our pending investigation."

"Give me his number. Come on Billy, let's get out of here and do some damage control."

Chief took a deep breath, relieved he'd dodged a cannon ball aimed right at his head.

On his way out Pines said, "One more thing, Harry. Next time you better clear it through me, or it'll be you in cuffs. Got it?"

"Got it, won't happen again."

He waited a few minutes then returned Steele's call.

"Joe, what's up?"

"I've been waiting here for over an hour, is everything okay?"

"I got detained by Pines, but he's gone. Why don't you go interview her? You can report back to me when you're done."

The Chief leaned forward and put his face in his hands. His bid for Attorney General just took a turn for the worse.

Tuesday, September 13, 2010 3:00 PM
Daniel Patrick Moynihan Court House, New York, NY

Hope and Stan arrived at the court house just as the proceedings began. They waited until the judge called my name before they approached the bench.

After reading the charges, Judge Paul Carter asked, "Mr. Green do you have counsel present?"

"Yes he does your honor. Hope Brennan, may I approach the bench?"

I turned around surprised. I'd heard Stephens and Ty were arrested at the same time, but I haven't been allowed to make any calls yet.

"Yes, make it quick, please," Judge Carter replied.

"If it pleases the court," Hope started, but Carter waved her off.

"Where are you from, Counselor?"

"Dix Hills your honor."

"Okay, I don't know what they do there. Here we keep it informal. State your piece, and we can move on."

"Yes, your honor. I'm here to represent Richard Green."

"How do you plead Mr. Green?"

"Your honor, I know you're busy, but could I have a brief moment with him before he answers?"

"Take your time," he said peering down at me. "We have all day."

We whispered to each another and then I said, "I plead not guilty your honor."

He looked at the state District Attorney, Robert Baines, who stated, "Due to recent activity we just learned, we request Rich Green be held without bail."

"Objection your honor," Hope blurted out raising her hands. "Mr. Green is a pillar in the community, and he should be released on his own recognizance. He is by no means a flight risk."

"Your Honor, we just learned he may be involved in other serious crimes against the State. We request he be held until we have time to investigate."

Hope looked at the DA and said, "I don't know how you do it here, but in Dix Hills we share discovery." She looked at Judge Carter, who smiled, "Your Honor, this is not proper. We were not alerted to any of this, and thus had no time to prepare. I request Mr. Green be released with the understanding he cannot leave the city, or whatever boundaries you feel are acceptable."

The murmur of the crowd grew louder by the second. Carter grabbed his gavel and slammed it down twice and restored order.

"District Attorney Baines, you know you can't just bring surprise evidence up for a crime the accused wasn't charged with at his arraignment."

"But your honor," he tried to interject.

"Do not interrupt me when I'm speaking," he said with firmness.

"I beg your pardon," he said, and nodded his head in respect.

"Mr. Green will be released under his own recognizance with the understanding he's to report any travel outside of New York City to the court before traveling."

"Any objections from either of you?" They both shook their heads. "Ms. Brennan, I suggest you brush up on our big city rules before you return. Trial is set to begin November 24, 2011. Next!"

"I'll wait for you outside," Hope said.

"Thanks, I'll be out as soon as possible."

***

They had me processed and out in less than an hour. Now to find Ms. Brennan. Who hired her, and what does she know about investor law?

I walked into the lobby where she sat next to a nerdy looking guy.

"Ms. Brennan? Thanks for your help today."

"No problem, that's what I do."

"Can we talk?"

"Sure, have a seat."

I looked at her, then at him.

"He's my partner Stanley, I mean Stan Lipkiss."

"Nice to meet you Stanley," I said. "What type of law do you practice?"

"I don't practice law."

"What do you do, Stanley."

"I help Ms. Brennan by uncovering interesting tidbits of information from well-hidden sources unseen by the human eye. I'm unrivaled at discovering things people wish to keep private."

I looked at him, then her, puzzled.

"He hacks computers."

"Let's get out of here before they come up with something else to charge me with."

"They can't just charge you without cause, Mr. Green."

I looked at her and thought, really?

"I'm kidding about the charges. I'm not kidding about getting out of here. Can you take me to my apartment? We can talk on the way."

"Sure. Can we stop on the way and grab dinner?" Stanley asked. "We're both starving."

"Good idea," I said. "Bring your car around and pick me up. I need to make a call."

They took off, and I dialed Rosa's number.

"Rich, is that you?" Rosa answered with an excitement in her voice I haven't heard in a while.

"Yes it is, Rosa. I'm so sorry about Monday. I'm sure you've heard by now..."

"Yes, Rich I heard. I have something to tell you."

"I've got a few things to tell you, and I need to go first, please."

"Okay, go ahead."

"First, I'm really sorry about the way I've treated you. Believe it or not, I want to take our relationship to the next level. I'd understand if you didn't want to after what happened."

"What do you mean by the next level?"

"You know, the next level." She didn't respond right away, and I began to regret saying it.

"The next level?"

"Yes, the next level. I've thought about it long and hard, and I'm ready."

"Explain the next level to me."

"I will, in person."

Hope and Stanley pulled up, and I jumped into the car.

"My ride's here. Can you come by tonight? I can't leave the city."

"Around 7:30?"

"Perfect, see you then."

Hope and Stan looked at each other before Stan said, "Where we eatin'?"

"Head toward FDR Drive going south. Follow it around the park to 9A. I know a great place."

I text Rosa, "Can u meet us at Luke's in 30 instead?"

"I'm not familiar with the city Mr. Green, just tell me where to turn."

"Call me Rich, will ya. Mr. Green makes me feel like I'm your dad or something. By the way, how long have you been practicing law, and who hired you?"

"I'm been a lawyer for almost a year now! And your wife Rosa asked me to help you today."

"Don't get me wrong, I appreciate you helping me today, but this case is going to get intense and my freedom's on the line. I kind'a need somebody who knows the in's and out's of securities rules. Maybe you can refer someone?"

"Yes, who's us?"

"Lawyer and nerdy sidekick."

"Mr. Green, I'll have you know I worked for Chief Moore for eight years before becoming a lawyer. I've been dreaming about a case like this. Getting the chance to beat him at his own game is what I want. I assure you, you're in good hands."

"Still, how many cases have you tried in your year?" I said accenting the word 'year' making quotation marks with my fingers.

"Tons of them, mostly small criminal cases."

"Tons?" Stanley asked.

"This isn't a small criminal case you know. The media will be hounding you every minute of the day. With an alleged murder case as well. This is serious stuff, there's no room for error."

I could see her frown in the mirror. However, she kept her chin up, showing her confidence.

"Murder charges? Is that what Baines tried to introduce?"

"There's nothing there that involves me. Let's get your friend something to eat, and we can talk some more. Take a left at the light and go up a few blocks. Luke's is on the right; we'll be meeting Rosa there."

"Great, she sounds like a wonderful person," Hope said.

"You two've never met?"

"Nope, just spoke over the phone. Her friend Martha referred me."

"Martha? The religious lady?"

"I guess you could call her that. Do you know her?"

"No, but Rosa has mentioned her several times. Are you religious?"

"I'm a Christian if that's what you're asking."

Now I have one more thing to discuss with Rosa.

Stan, being quiet for most of the ride, finally chimed in softly, "Let the games begin."

Tuesday, September 13, 2010 6:00 PM
Luke's Lobster, Williams Street, New York, NY

We pulled up to Luke's, and I jumped out of the car and headed straight in hoping Rosa had already arrived. She was sitting at the corner table waiting. She had her MBC and my Allagash Dubbel Reserve ready. I rushed over and gave her a passionate embrace.

"It's so good to see you," I whispered in her ear. I felt myself tremble, and wanted to cry, but held it back.

"It's good to see you too, Rich."

We stood there motionless, as if all time had ceased to exist.

We were quickly removed from this state as Stan announced his entrance with the classic, "Get a room, really."

"Rosa, allow me introduce Hope Brennan and her faithful sidekick Stanley."

"Stan!" he emphasized. "I go by Stan, thank you."

"Hi Hope, nice to finally meet you in person," Rosa gave her a warm hug. "Thank you so much for helping us out."

"No problem."

Rosa pointed to the chairs, granting permission for them to join us. Two portions of Noah's Ark waited to be devoured. Stan didn't need an invitation. He helped himself to the various seafood rolls and other stuff.

"Hey Julie, bring us another order, and drinks for these two."

She looked at me differently than normal—no smile, no emotion, just an "okay, coming right up." The comfort and warmth that made this place special disappeared.

"What's up with her?" I asked Rosa.

"Remember, I was here waiting on you when the news broke. They all saw it."

"May I get anything else for you guys?" Julie asked as she placed the basket and drinks on the table.

"Another helping of these," Stan replied pointing to the crab rolls. "They're awesome! What are they?"

"Crab rolls Stanley," I told him.

"So Hope, I understand you previously worked for the government?" Rosa asked.

"Yes I did. I left there to become a lawyer and defend those who need it. My insight on how they operate is a huge advantage. Believe it or not, Stan over here is an expert in gaining valuable information from unlikely sources. We'd really like to have the case."

"He hacks computers when he's not stuffing his face," I added.

"Technically, I'm not a hacker, per say," he said with a mouth full of crab roll, "more of a public domain researcher. The word hacker has such negative connotations. If there's information floating around, I'll find it."

The four of us talked for a few hours, getting to know each other. Hope's dedication to her God came through loud and clear. She made a compelling case why she should represent me, and how her faith and background would help. I still had my doubts though.

"Rich, I need to get back to the island," Hope said. "I've a busy day tomorrow. Before I leave though, we never discussed today's fees."

I looked over at Rosa and she shrugged her shoulders. I knew what she meant. Don't be cheap!

"What do I owe you?"

"I'll only charge you $2500 for today."

I smiled and nodded my head, "Can I send you a check?"

"Sure, send it tomorrow." She handed me her card and pointed at the bottom, "Here's my address. You can send it there."

"I'll send it first thing in the morning."

Hope and Stanley stood up, we shook hands and hugged, and off they went.

"I'll be in touch," Hope said as they left.

We paid the bill before Rosa and I hailed a cab and made the one mile journey back to my place.

★★★

"Where do we start?" Hope asked. "I'd like to have a solid plan before I call Rich."

"Do you still have an inside connection at the agency?" Stan replied.

"Yeah, I still hang out with a few of the guys. They'd never divulge anything though. The Chief would have their heads."

She remembers all too well seeing the Chief's clenched jaw and red face as he reprimanded anyone who had the gall to antagonize him. She can't imagine who'd risk their career to help her.

"Wasn't there one guy who was sweet on you? Carl or Chris, or something like that?"

"Cody? We were only friends, and we haven't spoken much since I left."

"Call him in the morning and ask him what he knows. I'll probe around and start the backgrounds on Rich and his buddies. In the meantime, I'm gonna get some shut eye. Drive safe."

She punched him in the arm and turned up the radio. Within minutes he kicked back and fell asleep. She spent the rest of the ride mind-mapping the process and building his defense. She wanted this case and prayed for guidance, and for God's will to prevail.

★★★

Everything changed since my arrest 24 hours ago. Instead of fighting to gain control of companies in an effort to destroy them, somebody is trying to gain control of my life in an effort to destroy me. I don't like the feeling.

I looked up, and Rosa was staring at me.

"Anybody home?" she asked waving her hand in front of my face.

"Yes, I'm sorry. It's been a trying couple of weeks. Can I get you anything to drink?"

"No thanks." She looked deep into my eyes, "Are you okay with me being here? You look distant."

"I got a lot on my mind, but I want you here with me, Rosa."

"You sure?"

"Absolutely, I do have a couple of things to discuss though. First is Hope. Do you think she can handle the case?"

"Why not?"

'Ya know she's..." I noticed myself scratching my neck, searching for the right words.

"She's an attractive woman?"

"No. I mean she is attractive, but that's not it. She's religious; will she be able to hold up under the pressure?"

"She seems capable to me, but it's your choice. I kinda like the idea of a Christian lawyer. Maybe she'll actually have scruples."

"I guess that's my concern. Will she be able to mount a solid defense on my part? Sometimes lawyers have to bend the rules a bit."

"Then be upfront with her from the beginning. Make sure she understands everything; not just most things, but everything. If she still accepts the case then proceed. The second thing?"

"My timing may be all wrong, but I need to ask anyway."

"What?"

I took a deep breath and waited for what seemed like an eternity, "Will you marry me, all over again?"

She gazed into my eyes and smiled. Her dark brown eyes and beautiful smile were the two things I noticed when we first met. They continue to be two of her best attributes. She laid her hands on top of mine and looked away. I'm about to be crushed.

"If you'd have asked me a month ago I'd jumped into your arms and let you take me away forever."

"But?"

"Things have gotten complicated."

"And?"

"I love you, but how can I be sure you're asking because you love me and want to spent the rest of your life with us?"

Us? What?

"Three weeks ago you weren't interested, now you are?"

"I was interested three weeks ago, and three months ago. I just didn't realize it. I love you Rosa."

"What about kids, and a family? Are you ready for that?"

"Yes, I am. Regardless of how this bogus lawsuit plays out, It's time for a new chapter in my, I mean our life. No more TV shows, no more trying to impress everybody by keeping up with Buffett. It's over. End of story. By the way, you said us earlier, what did you mean?"

"The three of us, you, me and," she pointed to her belly, "our baby. I'm pregnant!"

She started to cry, bringing tears to my eyes. I reached my arms around her slender frame and squeezed her like never before.

"I love you Rosa Milano."

"Rosa Green," she replied.

Wednesday, September 14, 2010 9:00 AM

My goal today is to meet with Hope and discuss the particulars of my business, and the case against me. Rosa has another full schedule of surgeries today, so she can't accompany me. It's been forever since I drove myself anywhere, not to mention all the way to Huntington Station. The drive will do me good.

I took a cab to my parking garage. I'll drive the STS today; the Carrera may give Hope the wrong impression. I fired it up and listened to the sweet sound of the Northstar engine. I love to hear it purr at idle, and grumble when I hit the gas. I punched Hope's address into the On-star and took off. I'd never find my way out of the city without it.

Once I got through the Queens Midtown Tunnel and onto the Long Island Expressway, I set the cruise. I drove past the high-rise apartments built right on top of each other. People stacked 50 stories tall. Wow, how do they do it?

I pulled into the complex housing Hope's office, a typical Long Island professional building, nothing like mine. Four stories, fully leased to Dentists, eye doctors, insurance agents, and lawyers. The lobby consisted of one elevator, three fake Ficus trees, and a glass encased, floor by floor listing of businesses, arranged by suite number.

Office 115 was located toward the back, away from the elevators on the inside of the building, wrapping around the overgrown courtyard. My guess is these are the cheapest offices. I noticed each office looked the same, at least on the outside. There were engraved name plates on each solid wood door, with a thin glass pane running vertically outside the door frame.

Before entering I spied through the glass. Stanley sat in what appeared to be the reception area, surrounded by enough monitors, keyboards, and various other gadgets to make any serious day trader feel inadequate. I leaned my head closer to the wall to view the other side of the office. Hope's office door was opened. She saw me looking through the window and waved me in.

"Hi Stanley," I said entering the office.

He pointed over his back with his finger pointing to Hope's office.

"What're you working on?" I asked him.

"Background stuff on you guys and what you do. Trying to get a better understanding of the government websites and how they operate. You never know when someone may need access."

"You never do know," I said, and headed into Hope's office. A quick scan showed off her conservative nature. Numerous Law books piled on tables and shelves. A few pictures hung on the walls, none with any man or children. She won't be burdened with family, giving her time to concentrate on my case.

She whispered for me to shut the door, which I did.

"Have a seat," she said. "I know my office isn't what you're used to, but it does the job. A good lawyer makes her mark in court anyway."

This is way better than the dump, but a far cry from our uptown office.

"Let's get started," she said. "If you don't mind, I'm recording our conversation. It may help down the road."

"No problem, I'm used to being recorded. Is Stanley joining us?"

"No. Stan is immersed in his own private world. Plus, he's not privileged to our conversations. So tell me, what's going on?"

Where do I start?

"Well, about four years ago my business struggled. Ty and I had a difficult time cultivating leads into potential takeover clients. Then I get this call from out of nowhere saying he had some good info for me. So I meet this guy, and he gives me the scoop on a company called Smithworth Industries."

She nodded her head along with me, anticipating my next statement.

"I considered it borderline insider information. Nothing that would've made any difference either way, except it gave me a slight advantage. I took it and made a small fortune."

"Then I hired a driver, Rasta, and he introduces me to Mark Stephens, my former lawyer. Rasta told me Stephens' specialty is securities law. He helped clear him of felony charges back home, and I should use him. We meet and have a lot in common so I put him on retainer."

"Go on," she said.

"I get another call from the same guy and he tells me about InCaHoots. This time the information is clear cut inside stuff. I confer with Stephens who tells me it's no big deal. He can get us around it. We put it in play, and we make another killing."

She looks at me with her right hand rubbing her chin.

"I seem to recall something about them. I'll have Stan check into that, go on."

"Then comes Diaboll, Inc. Same thing except more insider info and more money. I felt it's not right, but I figure my lawyer puts his approval on it, so I must be okay. And then we get to Sperry, Inc., which is being litigated as we speak. These four deals put me on the map as one of the big-time players on the street. I've been a regular on FNN and had my own show starting in a few weeks. Then of course I get arrested."

"So there is reason for these charges?"

"In a sense, yes. The crazy thing is we all do this. I didn't get any information that would really be considered insider. And the informant? It almost sounds like a set-up in the making."

"Why do you say that?"

"Too easy. The information handed over to me without anything expected in return. You'd think as much as I made, they'd have wanted some reward."

"Nobody ever asked you for anything in return?"

"Nope."

"Didn't that make you suspicious?"

"No, I figured they held a bunch of stock in these companies and made their profit when the stocks rose. Looking back on it, I feel like an idiot. They played me perfectly."

"Is there anything else I should know about?"

"Yes. Did you hear about a guy named Jack Harvey who was murdered a few days ago?"

She nodded.

"It turns out, he and Mr. X were one and the same. He'd also been blackmailing Ty. To complicate it further, someone identified Ty as the man seen standing over his dead body. He jumped into my driver's cab, and we've not seen or heard from either of them since."

"Mr. X?"

"The name he chose when he threatened me to do business with him or he'd go to the Fed's."

"Why did he blackmail Ty?"

"He'd been cheating on his wife, and Jack knew about it. Ty went to confront him in person, and then ran out of the building and jumped in the cab. My guy Reef saw it."

"So that's what the DA meant about other charges at your arraignment," she said.

"I don't believe Ty would do such a thing. His wife already knew about the affair, why would he kill him?"

"And you haven't heard from the cabbie, or Ty, since that day?"

"No, I haven't."

"For real? We have to be completely honest with each other. You've heard nothing from either of them since that day?"

"Not a peep from either one."

"Well on a positive note," Hope stated. "These cases take time to process. The prosecution will have a tough time trying to prove their case without solid, credible witnesses."

"Somehow we need to find them two," I said.

"Yeah, before the Chief does."

I sat back and thought about what she just said. Are they even still alive? Are they in this together?

"Do you think you can help me?"

"You did commit insider trading violations to some degree, so we'll have to get around that. As far as murder and obstruction of justice, we'll beat that without a problem." She hesitated for a moment, and raised her eyebrows saying "Provided you're innocent."

"Yes I'm innocent, already told you that."

"Then okay. All we need now is to fill out some paperwork and get started."

"I like your demeanor and style, but let me sleep on it. I'll call you by Friday with my answer. Fair enough?"

"Fine with me, but you'd better get someone quick. The Chief's boys aren't standing around waiting on you. Every hour you wait, is one more hour of advantage they gain."

Nice. She can hit hard.

"I'll be in touch. You have some spunk. I like that."

I got up, shook her hand, and exited the office. Stanley hadn't moved—his back toward the door with his head stuck between the monitors.

"See ya Stanley, have a wonderful day."

He gave me another finger wave and went back to whatever he was doing.

★★★

Rosa checked her schedule as she walked back to her office. Her next surgery wasn't for another two hours. She shut her door and sat in the recliner by the window. I have a lot to do over the next eight months.

"GM think'n of u! Have an appt Friday At 2 for ultrasound Do you want to go?"

She checked her email looking for the response from her Human Resource Department concerning FMLA. This would give her 120 days of unpaid leave upon birth of her baby. Her other request concerned reducing her position from full-time to per diem instead. Once the baby started school she'd reevaluate her options.

Her cell buzzed, "I'd love too, text me To remind me, love you."

Thursday, September 15, 2010 10:00 AM
Pine Street Office, New York, NY

Stephens, Reef Stantchin, and I met at my office, trying to figure out what happened. A week ago we're basking in the glory of another nice deal, now we're effectively out of business. As if insider trading and obstruction of justice isn't enough, the murder of Jack Harvey brings another serious issue to contend with, the looming possibility we'll be spending the rest of our day's behind bars.

"What do you make of all this?" I asked trying to break the deadlock of silence.

"We need to find Ty," Reef replied.

"No kidding. If he didn't kill Harvey, and I don't believe he did, he's got nothing to worry about. Why doesn't he make contact?"

"He's scared, that's why. The cops got the two things they need on him," Stephens added, "location and motive. If the eye witness is credible, he's screwed. We should start to distance ourselves from him. He's trouble."

I crossed my arms and reclined my chair. There's no way he's capable of killing anyone.

"Ty and I have been together for a long time, Mark, much longer than you and me, and I'm not abandoning him. Where's Rasta? He's disappeared off the face of the earth."

"My guys are all over that," Reef said. "Have you guys got lawyers yet?"

I looked at Stephens and he shrugged his shoulders.

"I can't represent either of you because I'm part of the suit," he said. "I'm using an old friend of mine, Robert Sawyer, he's willing to take us all on."

"No way," I said. "He's bad news, I'll pass."

"Do you have a better option?"

"Not yet, although the lawyer who bailed me out wants the case. Not much experience, but she worked under Chief Moore for eight years. She knows him and how they work over there."

They both looked at me with a fixed stare.

"What?" I asked.

"Suit yourself," Stephens said. "You need someone who'll do whatever it takes--legal or not."

I leaned toward him putting my palms down on the desk. "I think I'm done with that. From here on I'm playing it straight."

"It's too late for that, Rich," Stephens said. "Play it straight now and you'll be locked up forever."

"Maybe it's too late for you, but not me."

"What's your plan, Rich?" Reef asked. "Can I help?"

"I'm not sure yet," I looked at Reef, and stood up, walking toward the window. "A few things I am sure of; I'm not using Sawyer under any circumstance, period! I will need your help, Reef. We'll all need to stay in synch with each other, and we need to find Ty and Rasta."

"Keep your phone handy Mark, and report anything you find, I'll do the same," I said escorting him out to the elevator.

***

"Chief, we think we found the cab," Steele said. "Some hikers reported an overturned cab in a creek out on the Island matching the one Gillian got away in. I'm on my way."

"Good job, Steele. Report back to me at once." Chief already knew about the cab. Finding the driver became the Chief's top priority.

He signed on to the agency's secure browser and opened the search program, giving him access to phone bills, credit card statements, airline reservations, and just about any other piece of information ever recorded about anyone. He needed to be careful where he went because the sight is monitored by Internal Affairs. Once he signs out, an email is generated and sent to him and IA requiring an immediate response justifying the search. Since the cab was considered evidence, he had his entry point.

He typed in, "Andre St. Pierre" and waited for the results. Thirty-three hits, two of whom lived in New York. He knew which one he wanted, and clicked on the link opening his file. He glanced briefly through the records until he found the last known address. He jotted it down, along with the names of known accomplices he's been known to associate with. He signed off and headed out to tie up another loose end.

★★★

Reef Stantchin removed the mag-light from his belt and tapped it three times on the door of the small, one room apartment. His men did a great job of hacking motor vehicle files to find the address of the cab owner, who he suspected was Rasta. He hoped it would lead him one step closer to discovering the truth about Harvey's death.

He repeated his knock, and still no answer. He tried the door, but it was locked. He reached to his left and unfastened the lock pick set from his belt. Rich often teased him about being a super-hero with all his tools on his utility belt.

As he started the process to defeat the lock, he heard the elevator bell. He quickly removed the pick and walked away from the door, and hid in the stairwell entry. He removed his Yankee cap and slowly peeked around the corner, and saw two men approach the same door. After a few knocks, and still no answer, they looked at each other, shook their head, and unholstered their weapons. The second man kicked the door, forcing it open, and they entered.

Stantchin ran down the three flights of stairs and across the street to his car. He grabbed his camera, positioned himself out of sight, and waited for their exit. He'd take some pictures of them as they exited and then go back up to the apartment and have a look around himself. Although he's not sure what's happening, he knows he's headed in the right direction.

"Louie, head to the 500 block of w 144th now."

Stantchin spotted one of the men from upstairs exit the apartment, and stand by the door looking around. He waved to the other man who also exited carrying something resembling an envelope. They got into their car and headed away. He snapped off at least 20 pictures including the license plate from what is assured to be an unmarked police car.

"Reef, I'm in Jersey about 2 hours away."

"Never mind, thx."

Stantchin crossed the street and made his way back up to the third floor apartment. Either the tenant is a slob, or his predecessors ransacked the place. He put on his latex gloves and moved swiftly through the apartment, taking great care not to disturb anything. He couldn't find any trace of the resident. There weren't any bills, pictures, or anything else to see. He peeked his head out into the hall, making sure it was clear. He raced back to the stairwell and out to his car.

He drove off and parked a few blocks away to study the pictures he'd just taken. Digital cameras are an investigators best friend. He quickly scrolled through the shots of the two men without recognizing them. He took special notice of the last two pictures. He zoomed in on what the second man carried out—an envelope for sure. The next picture confirmed his guess. The government license plate indicated they are cops. He'll run the plate to determine the agency or precinct who owned the car. Then he'll be able to identify the men.

Friday, September 16, 2010 09:40 AM
Huntington Station, NY

Stan's work over the last few days encouraged Hope. She'd never seen anyone disable firewalls and other blockades with such ease. She was even more impressed with the information he found; so much for privacy anymore.

"Do you think I should call him?" she asked. "He said we'd talk today. Should I wait or call him?"

"Re-freaking-lax will ya," he replied. "He'll call, I promise."

"How do you know?"

"Don't worry about how--just be ready when he does. Look at what I found last night. You're gonna love it."

"What do you have?"

"Why don't you order a pizza while I get logged on."

No problem. He hasn't asked for anything other than food yet, praise God. I couldn't pay him in any other way at the moment.

"Did you hear that Rich proposed to Rosa after we left the restaurant?"

"Awwhhh, how sweet! But aren't they already married? And make it a large with Italian sausage and mushrooms, and an order of wings with hot sauce on the side."

On second thought, It may be cheaper to pay him in cash.

"Re-proposed then, is that better? And Rosa expecting gives us another reason to clear his name."

"Speaking of clearing names." He jumped out of his chair and gave her a hug. "I never did thank you for helping me back then. Thank you, Hope."

"I know you don't want to hear it, but thank the Lord. I was just His messenger," she said as he walked back to his desk.

He nodded and whispered, "I know."

★★★

"Reef, this is Rich, I got your message about the cab. Call me."

Then to Rosa, "r u sure Hope's the one?"

"Yes, Rich call her and get it started. Surgery in a few, call u after, love you!"

I started to dial Hope's number. I still feel uneasy and unsure about her ability to provide a proper defense, but one way or another I have to commit. If she doesn't work out, I won't have time to adjust.

"Hope Brennan's office."

I hung up. "I'm just not sure."

I called Reef. I needed another opinion.

"Hey Rich, got news for you concerning the cab," Reef said.

"Before we discuss that, I need your advice on hiring Hope Brennan. What do you think?"

"I don't know much about her. The fact that she worked under Moore may help, but her lack of experience may hurt. Do you have any other options?"

"Actually, no. Things are happening so fast and I've relied on Stephens in the past."

"With all due respect Rich, there's quite a lot riding on this, and timing is not in your favor. Regardless of who you retain, you better make a decision, and quick."

"Yeah, I know," I said. "Let me get this done and I'll call you back about Rasta later." End call.

My answer then appeared in black and white, "Do it Rich"

So I did.

"Is this Stanley?" I asked.

"This is Stan. Who's calling?"

"Rich Green, is Hope there?"

"Sure, I'll get her. . . Hope, Rich Green on line 1."

Goof ball could at least put phone on mute.

"Hi Rich, how are you," Hope answered.

"I'm doing okay, considering the circumstances."

"Stan and I've been working on your case, and there's a few things we must do immediately."

"What?"

"Before we get into that, can we discuss our relationship? Are you planning to retain us?"

"Yes, I've decided to give you your big break."

Before she could reply, I added, "With three stipulations. First, my private investigator, Reef Stantchin, runs the investigations. Second, if I feel you're in too deep, I have the right to find you help or get a new lawyer. Agreed?"

"What about Stan? He's part of my team."

"Stan's okay with me, provided he doesn't do anything stupid. He'll report to Reef. Agreed?

"Yes, I think that's fair. What's number three?"

"Your fees, what are they?"

"$50,000 upfront and $200 per billable hour thereafter, paid weekly."

"Really?" Her inexperience is showing.

"Yes, is that too much?"

"No, that's right in line with what I was thinking." She should be charging 10 times that. "Now what do we need to do immediately?"

"Petition the court to prevent the state from freezing your bank accounts. If they try this under RICO, they'll revoke your bail and break you financially."

Wow! That was $50,000 well spent. "What are you waiting for? Get on it, now! Please, that is. Sorry."

"One step ahead of you, my runner is already on his way with the petition. I'll call you early next week, or if anything comes up before then. When can I expect the retainer?"

"I'll mail you a check for half today and the other half in 30 days."

"I'll need the entire amount up front to take the case."

Commit one way or another, I told myself. The clock is ticking.

"Okay, Hope. I'll put in the mail tomorrow."

"How about if my runner picks it up in an hour?"

Nice, she's got some guts.

"I'll meet him at my apartment when he's done at the courthouse. Thanks Hope, we'll talk next week."

★★★

"Rich, call me"

"What's up Reef?"

"Several things. First, we tailed one of Moore's agents. A guy named Joe Steele, and he led us to the cab. Rasta ditched it on Long Island in some creek bed. We also found the name of the owner of the cab. An Andre St. Pierre. Is this Rasta's real name?"

"I don't know his real name."

Silence for a few seconds. He probably thinks I'm an idiot, surrounding myself with people I don't even know.

"Well anyway," Reef said. "When I got there he's not home, so I start to pick the lock. I get interrupted by two men who promptly kick the door in and ransack the place."

"Did they see you?"

"No, I hid when I heard them coming. Once they entered the apartment, I ran down to my car and took some pictures as they left. I went back up and checked the apartment, but didn't find anything."

"What about the men, who they are?"

"Reggie Dupree and Chief Investigator Harry Moore, both from the Attorney General's office."

My heart skipped a beat.

"The two clowns who arrested me?"

"One and the same. What do you suppose they're looking for?"

"Probably the same thing we are, Rasta!"

"Rich, as many times as you were in his cab, his name never came up," he asked again. "Aren't they supposed to have their ID badges on the dash?"

"I'm sure he did, I just never paid attention to it. It was always Rasta and Boss Man. Do you have any pictures of St. Pierre?"

"Not yet. I was hoping to find one in his apartment. There's nothing in his motor vehicle file, and he has no license."

"A cabbie with no license and no photos?" Now I am a confirmed idiot.

He didn't respond.

"Call Hope," I said. "Her partner Stanley claims to be a computer genius. Says he can find out anything about anybody. Maybe he can track this guy down?"

"My guys are real good, Rich."

"I know they are, but test him. See if he's as good as he says. I'll text you his number in a few. By the way, have you found anything on Ty?"

"No, he's still running around with Rasta."

"Quiz Stanley about that as well. Maybe he's got an angle."

I put on my walking shoes, synced my blue-tooth, and headed down to the esplanade. Instead of my usual south bound trek toward Battery Park, I made my way north toward Rockefeller Park, which is two miles from my apartment. Me and Rich, Jr. will be spending many afternoons there.

On the way, I took in all the sights, sounds, and the rich, but not always pleasant, bouquet of the big city. Nothing will be taken for granted ever again. My freedom is at stake. Couple that with a wife and soon to be child on the way, and there's no playing around. Hope better perform!

On my way up, I always stop at the North Cove Marina. This is where my yacht will be docked. There are some beautiful ships here.

Once I reached the park, I turned around, heading back south toward my apartment. On the way back I stopped at pier 25: sand volleyball, an unbelievable miniature golf course, a lawn area for picnics, and children's playground jetting out into the Hudson. Whoever dreamt of transforming an old decrepit pier into a sports peninsula was brilliant.

As I left the pier, a young man handed me a pamphlet. Usually I just raise my hands and walk by without paying any notice, today though, I took it. I glanced at the cover. The big bold print jumped off the page at me, "Tired of Being Rundown, Find Restoration through Jesus Christ."

I shoved the pamphlet in my pocket and headed back home. As I passed by the marina on my way back, I thought about Ty--why hadn't he called me yet.

★★★

Hope watched in awe as Stanley began devouring the pizza and wings.

"Do you mind saving a slice for me?"

He motioned for her to come now before it's too late. She scooted her chair over to his desk and grabbed a slice and two wings.

"So tell me what you found last night."

He mumbled, nodded his head, wiped the hot sauce from his hands, and stretched his fingers like a pianist would before a concert.

"Would you come on already!" She said.

"You're always in such a hurry, relax. I'm warming up."

She raised her brow and stared at him.

"All right," he said, and lifted his hands in defeat. "I ran the backgrounds on Rich and his boys. It seems that while Rich is clean on the surface, the others," he said shaking his head with his nostrils flared, "not so much."

"Really?" she leaned in toward him.

"Ty has a few misdemeanors to his credit. Disturbing the public, bounced checks, those kinds of things."

Hope tracked right along.

"By the way, his credit score's worse than mine," he said laughing.

"Pretty bad, huh?"

"You don't have to agree. Let's move on."

"Mark Stephens is a whole other story. He's a piece of work. Has some anger problems, especially with the ladies. Been arrested many times for beating on his professional dates. If you know what I mean?"

"Well, they did arrest him at a strip club..."

"At least he's consistent. But here's the kicker. In 2003, he was indicted on several counts of securities fraud."

"I better ask Rich when he and Stephens started working together."

"His file, which is supposed to be suppressed," he gave me the wink, "shows charges were dropped. You may want to dig into this more."

"Why would they drop charges on him?"

"Good question, maybe he gave somebody up in exchange for immunity."

"Call Rich's guy Reef. I bet he can help clear this up."

"I don't need any help. I'm perfectly capable myself."

"I need your help on this, Stan. Put your pride aside and work together. You two are gonna make an awesome team, thanks."

She smiled at him and leaned back in her chair. It's time to make contact and call in a favor.

"Hey, I no its been awhile, coffee?"

Friday, September 16, 2010 11:40 AM
Rectore Place, NY

Reef buzzed me from the lobby and I let him up. I unlocked the door and stepped into the bathroom to wash up real quick.

"Yo, Rich, you here?"

"Yeah, come on in. I'll be with you in a second," I yelled at him. "The coffee's fresh, help yourself."

I heard the familiar sound of the spoon clanking the side of the mug.

"I spoke with your boy, Stan," he said. "He's a weirdo, but he told me a few things I never knew. He may be as good as advertised."

I quickly dried off and rushed out into the kitchen.

"What?"

"Did you know Mark Stephens has been arrested numerous times for assault?"

"Assault? A few DWI's maybe, but not assault."

"He likes to beat up his hookers," Reef said. "Did you know he was indicted on several counts of securities fraud seven years ago?"

"No, I didn't. Where did you hear this?"

"Our boy Stanley discovered it."

"Now he's our boy," I said. "Something just isn't right. How can he still practice law? He should've been disbarred."

"Good question," Reef said. "He must have made a deal for immunity, otherwise you're right. He'd have lost his licenses and banned from law and securities."

I poured a cup of coffee. Reef followed me out to the balcony. I put the coffee on the pub table and rubbed my face with both hands. This just keeps getting crazier and crazier.

"Where does it end, Reef?"

He returned a puzzled look, and I nodded my head.

"On a positive note," he said. "Congratulations!"

"For what?"

"For what? Getting your relationship straight with Rosa, and having a baby!"

"Let's hope he has a father who's not in jail."

We both sat quietly. I don't know what he thought, but I couldn't get my mind off how awful it would be to be locked away, especially with a new family. The case felt like an albatross on my shoulders. Having a new PI, and an unknown for a lawyer didn't relieve much weight.

My phone vibrated, "Call me, luv u"

"What's the latest on Ty?" Reef asked.

"Nothing, what about Rasta? Any updates?"

"I put Stan the man on it."

Stan the man. And a lawyer named Hope. Gives me an idea.

"Let's go pay them a visit" I said. "Check out her operation, and you can get to meet Stan the man."

"Let's do it."

I dialed her cell.

"Hope Brennan's office how may I help you?" Her bright and cheery voice is incredible. I bet she sounds the same way even when mad.

"Hi Hope, this is Rich. We're headed out to see you and Stan. We'll be about an hour."

"Sure come on out, we'll be waiting." End call.

We left my apartment and jumped into his car. We stopped at the deli to grab a bite to eat on the way out to Long Island.

"I have a question for you, Reef. Have you ever prayed about stuff?"

He shot a quick puzzled look at me.

"That's a random question, but yes, of course."

"I mean really prayed? Not just saying grace before Thanksgiving."

"I'm sure I have, at one time or another, why?"

"How about God? Do you believe in God?"

"Yes, I believe there's a God out there, somewhere. I haven't given much thought to it over the last few years, why do you ask? I took it you are not a God kind of guy."

"You're right."

"Then why do you ask?"

I pushed my head back into the seat feeling apprehensive about sharing my feelings with Reef. I've always been the strong, unemotional guy. Now I feel weak and vulnerable.

"Hope was referred by Rosa's religious friend," I said. "And with a kid on the way and all, thought there might be a connection somehow."

His puzzled look returned.

"You know Rich, there's always a connection between God's will and man's actions."

"You believe that?"

"No doubt about it. One day I'll explain it to you."

I never pegged Reef to be into God.

We grabbed our hoagies and started out toward the Queens Midtown Tunnel. On the way I called Rosa.

"Hey baby got your text, what's up?"

"I'm ready to go to the doctors for my weekly checkup and ultrasound. Are you on your way to get me?"

Crap!

"What time is your appointment?"

"Two o'clock. You forgot about it, didn't you?"

"No. I mean yes. I did forget. I'm sorry, we're on our way to see Hope and Stan, but I'll reschedule and come get you."

"Don't worry about it. I'll just catch a cab." She hung up. Son of a gun, I did it again.

"Rich," Reef said. "Take my car, and I'll grab a cab. I'll call Hope and explain. We can meet later at the dump. There are some things I need to talk to Mark about anyway."

"You sure?"

"Yeah, go get her." He pulled over and got out. He leaned through the window. "Well? What are you waiting for?"

I slid over to the driver's seat and called Rosa. As soon as she picked up I said, "I'm on the way. I'll be there in 15 minutes."

"Thanks," she said sounding less than enthused and hung up.

I pulled out into traffic taking a page from Rasta's play book. As expected the horns blew, tires squealed, and the adjectives flew at me from all directions. I looked straight ahead as if it would forgive me, and accelerated toward the hospital.

My phone buzzed, Rosa calling back. I looked around insuring no cops would see me answer the phone.

"Yeah baby," I said.

"Don't worry about it Rich," she said.

"I'm on my way right now. I'll be there shortly."

"Really, Rich. It's okay, don't worry about it," she said. "I'm not mad; just take care of your business."

"Now I really feel bad, Rosa. I'm sorry; I want to be there for you."

"How's this? Come pick me up at 3. I'll be done by then. Okay?"

"You sure?"

"I'll see you at 3. Don't be late."

"I said I'm sorry."

"Just kidding, love you."

"Love you, too," I said. "3 o'clock it is." End call.

***

Reef arrived at the dump, catching Stephens walking down the stairwell to the street.

"Where you headed?" Reef asked.

"Out to the Hampton's--as usual," he replied.

"There are a few things I need to discuss with you. Can we go back to your office?"

He looked at his watch, then back at Reef. Then back at his watch.

"I really need to go. I have to get back to my apartment and pack."

No way he's going to blow off Reef.

"I'll share your cab," Reef said. "We can talk on the way."

He mumbled something before agreeing non-verbally. Reef hailed a cab, and they got inside. Stephens gave the driver his address, and he took off in typical cabbie fashion, high-speed and reckless.

"What do you want, Reef?"

"I noticed a major shift in your attitude since the arrest. What gives?"

He started to fidget and looked out the window.

"Well?"

"I just got arrested," he replied. "How'm I supposed to act? Happy and ecstatic?"

"No, just seems like you absolved yourself from Rich when he needs you the most, that's all."

"This is serious, Reef. My career and my freedom are on the line here. You, on the other hand, have nothing at stake."

"What does that have to do with anything?"

"Regardless of the outcome, you walk away, Reef," he replied. "You're safe. Rich and I may not get so lucky."

"Thats why I'm here today. To finc out what I can do to help you, but you seem unwilling to work together on this. Not the way a well paid lawyer on retainer should be acting."

"I told you two, I'm no longer working with or for Rich," He replied. "The time has come to part ways and save my ass."

"Is that why you hired your dirt bag lawyer friend? He'll do anything or screw anybody to win. He's facing disbarment in Jersey for his behavior and unethical habits."

Stephens looked at Reef and choked out a nervous laugh while shaking his head.

"You don't get it do you?" he shouted. "Lawyers are supposed to do that. That's what we get paid to do. We get paid to win cases, precisely why Rich hired me four years ago. Protect his butt at all costs. And we're in New York. I don't give a crap about Jersey."

"I don't agree with win at all costs. If so, where does it end? Someone has to be willing to do what's right every now and then."

"Well maybe you and miss goody-two-shoes Brennan, or whatever her name is, can fill that role. As for me, I know how the law works, and I'll exploit it every chance I get."

"I know what happened a few years ago," Reef said. "Something's going on with you, and I'm going to find out what it is?"

"What are you talking about," he asked. "A few minor assault charges, so what!"

"That's not what I'm talking about Mark," Reef replied. "What I'm talking about is much worse, like securities fraud."

Stephens leaned over the front seat, "Hey buddy, pull over at the corner."

On the way out, he reached into his wallet and grabbed a few singles and tossed them over the seat onto the cabbies lap. "See you round, Reef," he said. "It was nice."

He got out and scurried toward his place, looking like a hungry rat searching for cheese. I gave the cabbie my address and he took off back downtown.

"Rich, I'll be home. Call me when done."

★★★

I parked in the paid parking since I'm driving Reef's car. Grabbing the summer bouquet of flowers from the passenger seat, I headed in to surprise Rosa. Unlike the super elevator at my office, this one takes forever. When it finally came down to the lobby and opened up, I nearly got trampled by the exiting riders. Once they made their way past me, I spotted Rosa standing in the back--crying.

I entered the elevator, put her flowers down, and pulled her to me.

"What's wrong, baby?" I asked her as the new set of riders entered.

"Let's get out of here and go talk somewhere private," she replied.

"These are for you," I said, handing her the beautiful summer bouquet of daffodils, baby breath, and roses. A heart-shaped balloon stuck out above them reading, "To the world's best future Mother, I Love You!"

"Thanks," she said grabbing the vase. "Can you bring me back to the office? I need to get my car."

"Of course," I said. "So, what happened? Why the tears?"

She took a deep breath before answering, and sat down on the bench in the lobby.

"There's going to be complications with the birth," she said, "maybe more serious than I thought."

"What do you mean more serious than you thought? When did you know there'd be problems?"

She sat there motionless. Her arms wrapped tightly around her chest. I wanted her to answer, but didn't want to push her away either.

After what seemed an eternity she whispered, "Eclampsia is the name of the condition. By itself, it's easy to deal with. When mixed with pregnancy, it could get complicated."

"How complicated?"

"I'll find out in a few days once the tests come back," she said. "He thinks I may have a rare strain."

"And?"

Tears welled up again in her deep saddened eyes. I wanted to cry just looking at her.

"If I do, it isn't treatable, and most likely to cause death to either, or both of us, at delivery."

"What?" I stood up and walked to the window as if the answer was outside. I tried to gather my composure and walked back over to her, "Are you serious?"

"Yes, I am," she replied. "Do you think I'd make this up?"

Think before responding. Prove to her I'm changing.

"Sorry, I didn't mean it like that. What can we do about it?"

"Nothing at the moment. Once the tests come back and we know the severity, we'll know our options."

"Assuming the worst, Rosa. What is the worst case scenario?"

I felt the tears start to form. When was the last time I cried?

"Like I said, we can terminate the pregnancy, or we can hope for the best. Either way it's not good."

"What do you mean, hope for the best?"

"Try to give birth and hope we make it through," she said. "I'm not at all interested in terminating the pregnancy."

"But if you don't, then you and the baby may die anyway?"

"It's quite possible."

"I'm not saying I agree, disagree, or what to do. I'm just asking, okay?" I paused a few seconds. "If the baby will die anyway, why risk your life? We can try again."

"We can try, but most likely we'll get the same results," she said. "It's genetic and will happen each time I get pregnant. There's just no way I can live with myself knowing I gave up the baby. I can't do it."

I reached for her hand, and helped her stand. I pulled her close and hugged her tight, her frail body trembling with fear.

"I love you, Rosa. We'll get through this together."

She forced a smile.

"Thanks," she said. "I need to get back to the office."

Not the response I hoped for. Under the circumstances, and the way I've been, it's understandable. I've got plenty of work to do in this relationship.

Neither of us said a word until we pulled up in front of the medical plaza where she offices.

"I'm not sure what to say other than I respect your rights and opinion," I said. "What can I do to help?"

"Just love me," she said. "Make me feel special, even if I can't provide you with children. I know this may be hard for you, but that's what I need from you."

"Forever, Rosa, forever."

"Are you sure, Rich," she asked. "This could be your chance to walk away once and for all."

"What's that supposed to mean?"

She looked me dead in the eyes. I could see her pain.

"You've made it clear how you feel about children and marriage. Have you really changed?"

I lifted my hand about to answer.

"Don't answer," she said. 'Don't you dare answer... with words. You'll answer with your actions. If what you said to me over the last few days is real, it'll show."

"It is," I said.

She put her finger on her lips, "No words."

She got out and came around the front of the car to my side.

"I'll come by later and pick up the flowers," she said. "Thank you, they're beautiful." She gave me a kiss on the cheek and walked away.

Wow, another punch to the gut. Two months ago, I'm riding high, now my whole world is collapsing.

Tuesday, September 20, 2010 10:00 AM
Daniel Patrick Moynihan Court House, New York, NY

Hope walked into Judge Carter's chamber with a swagger. She expected to win a quick, easy approval, eliminating any chance of the state invoking RICO statutes. Seated across the typical government-issue large dark oak table sat DA Baines, and a well dressed older woman she hadn't met. To her left was Judge Carter, and to her right, Chief Harry Moore. Seeing him startled her. She took a step backward. Her swagger disappeared.

"Ms. Brennan," Chief said as he stood up to shake her hand, "been a while. How you been?"

"Just fine, thanks," she replied, forcing a smile as she took a seat at the other end of the table. She wasn't expecting to face off with him this early in the process.

"I see you two have already met," Carter stated. "Counselor Brennan, I believe you know DA Baines?"

They each gave the customary head-bob in respect.

"And seated across from you is Betty Rogers. She'll be doing the reporting."

Another head-bob in acknowledgment.

After Carter spoke the customary opening and we were sworn in, he said, "District Attorney Baines, please proceed."

"Your Honor, we'd like to enact the RICO statutes on Rich Green. He's being charged with serious crimes including securities fraud, extortion, and accomplice to murder."

"Extortion and Murder?" Hope blurted out.

"Quiet, counselor," Carter snapped. "Your time will come. Proceed Baines."

"As I was saying, your Honor, Mr. Green is suspected of serious crimes, and the State moves for him to be tried under RICO. The state also moves to revoke his bail."

Carter looked at Hope and waved his right hand slightly. She accepted this as her cue to begin.

"Your honor, up to this point Mr. Green has only been charged with securities violations and obstruction of justice, which is yet to be even remotely proved. RICO is not imposed under the nature of the alleged violations. Even though the crimes you state are serious, there's been no evidence provided to tie him to the charges, nor revoke his bail."

Carter looked at Baines waving his left hand away from Hope.

"Your Honor, his accomplice, who by the way is missing, has been identified by an eye witness at the murder scene. We can't let a murderer back on the streets."

"He's accused of securities violations, most of which are minor. Not murder," Hope interjected. "When you formally bring your charges against my client, with proof, we can discuss RICO and revocation of bail. Until such time, your honor, there's no basis."

"Chief Moore, do you care to respond?" Carter asked.

"We started Operation Geronimo last July, your Honor, and we've mounted an airtight case against Green Enterprises, including Gillian, and their lawyer Mark Stephens. My concern with this Green character is he tries to flee or worse, commits another crime against the great state of New York."

The only sound was Rogers banging away on her laptop.

"He's a snake, your honor," Moore continued. "He's devious and will stop at nothing to cover his tracks."

Carter looked back at me.

"Your honor, Rich Green and Ty Gillian have spotless records. Plus the precedent has already been set in this case allowing a criminal to avoid posting bail." She wasn't sure what type of reaction she'd get from this type of accusation toward the court, but had to protect her client.

"What do you mean, Brennan?" Carter asked. "If you're suggesting my court is playing favorites, you'd better be ready to prove it."

"Your Honor, I'm not suggesting anything of the sort. What I am saying is, Mark Stephens has been convicted on several counts of abuse, and also been indicted on serious securities violations years ago, and he posted bail. My client has no priors and should be allowed the same."

Hope stole a quick glance to gauge Chief's reaction, which went from arrogant to nervous. Nobody spoke.

"How can we revoke bail on Rich Green," Hope continued. "When we granted bail to a known felon accused of similar charges?"

Carter lifted his palms up looking at Baines, then Moore.

Baines went first, "I had no idea of such charges, your honor."

"You didn't know about any of the charges?" Hope countered.

"No," Baines replied. "I mean yes, I knew about the assault charges, but nothing about any securities fraud."

"Those charges were dropped four years ago, and they are irrelevant your Honor," Moore answered, obviously shaken. "I'd like to know how you found out about those Ms. Brennan."

"Your Honor, based on the fact the State already released Stephens without doing any background, my client, Rich Green, should to be tried as the charges state. No RICO, and no revocation of his bail."

Carter noticed the Chief's piercing stare toward Hope.

"Is there a problem, Harry?" Carter asked him. "You look... angry."

He lifted his hands and mouthed, "No problem here."

"Based on the comments from each party, my decision is that Rich Green stays out on his own recognizance. Until you bring sufficient evidence to this court showing his involvement in the other crimes, he'll be tried under the proper statutes for securities violations. No RICO action at this time. He'll be scheduled to appear back in court in three weeks. Each of you will receive notice of the exact date and time. You're all dismissed."

As they headed out of the room, Carter caught Hope's attention and motioned for her to stay behind.

"Close the door," he said. She did, and walked back to the table where he was still seated.

"Yes, your honor?"

"Sit down," he said pointing to the chair next to him. "This is off the record, please listen carefully. Chief Moore doesn't play games. He hates being shown up like you did to him today. He won't go away without a fight, tread lightly."

"Thank you, your Honor. I won't take your advice lightly."

"I'm serious," Carter stated again.

"I know you are. In case you didn't know, I worked under him for eight years before leaving the agency last year. I've seen him in action. Facing him today reminded me what he's capable off. Anything else?"

"You're free to go counselor," he said, and walked with her toward the door. "Good job today. You're about to get a lifetime worth of experience in one case--be ready."

"I will your honor. Thank you." She walked away, her swagger returned. She looked up to the sky, "Thank You Jesus!" She turned her cell on and called me.

"How'd it go?"

"Great, no RICO and no revocation of your bail."

"Thanks."

"You're welcome, but you need to thank the Lord. He's the one with His hand over us."

Tuesday, September 20, 2010 2:00 PM

"Hope Brennan's office may I help you?"

"This is Reef Stantchin, I work with Rich Green. Is Stanley in?"

"This is Stan!"

"Okay Stan. This is Reef. Do you have a minute? I need your help on a project."

"Sure, what' do ya got?"

Reef shook his head,. "Find out everything you can on a guy named AnDre St. Pierre."

"Okay, there'll probably be quite of few of them. Can you give me more to go on?"

"We believe he worked as a cabbie that Rich used for the last few years. He's Jamaican, and probably lives in the city."

"You think he's involved in the case in some way?"

"Yeah," Reef replied. "He was at the murder scene the same time Ty was there. In fact, he picked Ty up from the building as he fled. We haven't heard from either of them since."

"Do you have a picture of him by chance?"

"No, we don't. If you come across one, we could sure use it."

"Have you checked the motor vehicle website to view his license?"

Of course I did. I'm not a rookie.

"Yes, but according to them he doesn't hold any kind of license."

"What else do you know about him?"

"Other than driving a cab and being Jamaican, nothing."

"Is he the guy driving the Jamaican Flag Rich talked about?"

"We think it's the same guy."

"Okay, Reef, no problem. What's the best number to reach you?"

Reef gave him the number and ended the call. His next call started with *67 hoping it would generate an answer.

After a few rings a woman answered, "Hello, Ty?"

This may be tough, Reef thought to himself, "No, but don't hang up."

"Who is this?" she asked.

"My name is Reef. I'm a private investigator, and a friend of Ty Gillian's. We're trying to locate him. Have you heard from him lately?"

"No," she said. "Why would I have heard from him?"

Really?

"Let's start with you answered his cell phone," Reef said. "Look, I know about your involvement with him, and couldn't care less. I just need to find him before the police do. Since you have his cell phone, I figured I'd start with you."

"Well I haven't heard from him since the police broke down my door and ruined my marriage. When you finally track him down, let him know I'm okay. And I'll see him in court." End call.

Reef left his office and headed over to see Barbara Gillian. He couldn't understand what led Ty to cheat on her. She had everything a man could want in a woman; warmth, beauty, a solid family supporting her. But he knew there's always two sides to every failed relationship. He's investigated many of them. The picture perfect wife may also be hiding a brutal past, or living a secret life. He knew better in this case.

***

"It's time we make contact," Ty said. "I need to let my wife know I'm alive, even if she doesn't want to talk, at least she'll know. Plus Rich deserves to know what happened back there."

"Let's find a pay phone, though. They're probably tapping the phone lines and will trace the call back to the cell GPS locator."

"Not if we disable it." He grabbed the phone from Rasta's hand and went to work on the settings. Handing it back, "There you go, the GPS is disabled, but it will show last known location. We need to move along anyway. Let's go."

They jumped in the rental they had secured using a reloadable credit card and one of Rasta's fake ID's.

"I'm tired of hiding," Ty said. "I didn't do anything wrong, and I surely didn't kill anybody. I should turn myself in."

"Don't do that, man. Give me time to think it through."

"What do you mean? What's there to think through?"

"There's more to me than driving a cab, man."

Ty smiled not knowing what to expect. "Like what?"

"Like I work for Chief Moore."

Ty jammed on the brakes skidding off to the shoulder, "You what?"

"For the last four years or so," Rasta replied, picking the cell phone off the floor board. "Are you trying to kill us?"

"What did you do for him?"

"I spied on you guys, and reported to the Chief, man."

"Why you piece of . . ." Ty shouted, but decided to hold off. "And let me guess, when you realized what great guys we were you had a change of heart?"

"Sort of, man."

"Oh, really."

"This was before I saw how he operated," Rasta replied. "That's why I picked you up from Jack's building. You think it was a coincidence that I just happened to be driving by at that exact moment."

"I wondered about it, that's for sure. But you're still a piece of . . ."

Rasta held up his hands. "There's much more you should be wondering about. I'm in this way too deep. I need to get as far away from here as possible."

Ty grabbed Rasta's phone and dialed his wife, being sure to punch *67 to restrict the caller ID.

"Hello," Barbara said.

"It's me, can you talk? Barb are you there, don't hang up."

"I'm here."

"Look, I know you're mad. You probably don't even want to talk with me right now, and I don't blame you. I've treated you like crap, and you deserve better, but I need your help."

"What?"

"Two things. I need you to get in touch with Rich. His number is in..."

"I know his number, what's the second thing?"

"Tell him I'm with Rasta. I'll call him at Reef's office this evening at 7 PM. Will you do that?"

"What else?"

Man she's short.

"I'm sorry for putting you through such a mess. I really am sorry. When this whole thing settles I'd like to make amends with you. Try to make fresh start."

"Really? What about your child and its mother? Are you looking to make a fresh start with them as well?"

I could hear the hurt in her voice.

"You crushed me, Ty. Not only did you sleep with another woman, but you got her pregnant as well. Since we can't have kids, you go find someone who can. I'll give Rich the message, but it's too late for us. We're done. Goodbye."

Ty flipped the phone back to Rasta.

"That didn't sound too promising, man," Rasta said.

"Shut up, Man."

"Let me drive, I don't feel like getting killed today."

***

Reef parked his Buick Lacrosse a few houses down from the Gillian residence.

Stick to business, Reef, in and out. No staring, no games, strictly business. He took in a couple of deep breaths and knocked on the door.

"Who's there?" He hesitated before answering, almost walking away. Strong, be strong.

"Reef Stantchin. May I come in?"

The door opened just enough to pull the security chain taught. She closed it again and removed the linkage, and let him in.

"Hi Reef," she said. "It's been a while, how've you been?"

"I'm doing well. And you?" He never saw her look this drained. Her bloodshot eyes and unkept hair revealed her hurt.

"There've been better days in my life," she said. "I'm sure you already know about Ty and his affair."

He nodded as he looked around the apartment, trying not to make eye contact.

"That's why I'm here, Barb. I need to find him, have you heard from him?"

"As a matter of fact we just spoke, he asked me to tell Rich to be in your office at 7 PM tonight. He's going to call you guys. And that he's with Rasta? Or something like that. Probably one of his girlfriends."

"No, Rasta is the cab driver who picked him up the other day. We've been wanting to find both of them."

He punched in Rich's number. "Rich, b at my office at 7. Ty to call. Don't call me back, will meet u there."

"Well you won't have to look much further after to-night." She forced a smile.

"Why's that? Did he say anything?"

"Nothing worthwhile," she replied. "Can I get you a drink?"

The nervous feeling started bubbling in Reef's belly. He wanted to stay, but needed to leave. Hoping she'd convince him otherwise.

"I should probably get going."

"Do you still enjoy scotch?" she asked, walking to the cabinet next to the bookshelf. "Is G en Livet 18 still your favorite?"

She grabbed the bottle and took it to the kitchen, grabbed two large tumblers, and fixed two drinks. "On the rocks, just like old times." She said, handing the glass to him, making sure their fingers made contact. She smiled,

"Here's to an awful past, and a bright future, starting to-day."

He half-heartedly raised his glass in honor. Before drinking, he slowly moved his hand circularly to mix the drink and get a whiff of the wonderful bouquet. After a small sip he placed the drink on the table.

"I should probably leave," he said. "I'm sure you have a lot on your mind."

"Please don't go just yet," she said. "Let's talk about the old times. Get our mind off our troubles."

I don't have any troubles. Yet!

She got up from her chair and sat next to him on the couch.

He took another sip, a much bigger sip. The slight burn of the premium single malt scotch flowing from his lips to his stomach soothed his anxiety. This is all wrong.

Tuesday, September 20, 2010 6:50 PM
Newburgh, New York

Rasta drove up in front of the local coffee shop they chose to call Rich from. Ty exited the car and started toward the shop.

"Let's go, Rasta," Ty shouted. "We need to make the call and get moving."

"Tell Boss Man I'm sorry about all this."

"You can tell him yourself in five minutes. Come on let's go."

"Sorry man, I'm out." He hit the accelerator and took off like a rocket.

"Wait!" Ty yelled as he drove off.

Ty stood there not believing what just happened. He searched the strip center for a pay phone since Rasta took off with the cell. Not seeing one, he entered the coffee shop hoping they'd have a phone he could use. He noticed the patrons were cut from a different mold than his accustomed city dwellers.

"May I help you," the young lady asked. Her attractiveness caught Ty off-guard. He couldn't help but stare at the facial piercings she flaunted.

"Umm, yes," he replied. "Do you by chance have a pay phone?"

"A what?" She stared at him like he was from a different planet.

"You know, a pay phone. One of those things you put quarters in to make calls."

"I know what a pay phone is, just haven't been asked about one in forever." He noticed the huge bolt looking object inserted in her tongue as she spoke. I wonder if that hurt?

"Do you know where one is?"

She took a few steps away from the counter and yelled into the back room, "Scooter, do you know who has a pay phone? This guy out here needs one."

It felt like the whole crowd stopped what they were doing and focused on me.

"If it's a local call let him use our phone" he shouted back at her.

"Is it a local call?"

"No, but I can call collect." Ty scratched the side of his head. Is there still such a thing as collect calls anymore?

She gave me another strange look.

"Hey Pal."

I turned to look in the direction the voice originated.

"The gas station across the street has one," a young man wearing a weird stocking cap said.

Ty raised his hand about to thank him, "It even takes credit cards." He looked at his friends around the table. "We take credit cards in our town now, ever hear of them?" They all busted up laughing.

Ty gave him a fake smile as he left the shop.

★★★

By the time Reef pulled up to the curb outside his office, my stress level peaked. I got out of my car and approached him before he could exit.

"Where've you've been, Reef," I asked. "I've been waiting almost an hour."

"Something came up and I couldn't break away. I'm really sorry."

Reef has always shot straight with me so I didn't press him any further on his lateness. I smelled alcohol on his breath, which concerns me. He'd been through the 12-step program twice that I know of already.

"Reef, you okay?"

"I'm fine, why?"

"You're late for a important call, and you've been drinking?"

"I had one glass of scotch with Barbara. I'm good."

With Barbara? I'm not believing what I'm hearing. Is everyone around me nuts?

We entered Reef's office and saw the red LED on his answering machine blinking; missed calls, but no messages.

"Nice job Reef," I said. I plopped myself on to the couch.

He sat on his recliner and leaned back, eyes closed and his fingers tapping in rhythm on the arm rest.

"Do you want a cup of coffee while we wait to see if Ty calls again?" I asked him.

"I'll take a another drink," he replied.

"You sure that's a good idea?"

"I'm a big boy Rich. It's in the cabinet above the coffee maker. Help yourself to whatever you want."

I grabbed the half-emptied bottle of cheap scotch from the cabinet. I put a paper coffee cup upside down over the neck and sat it on the table in front of him.

"Talk to me, Reef" I said returning back to make some coffee. "What's going on?"

★★★

Ty walked back across the street to the sports bar located on the opposite end of the strip mall from the cafe. He'd get a drink and a burger before calling Barbara back. Did she give them my message?

The Front Page gave the appearance of any other sports bar. Plenty of flat panel televisions broadcasting a myriad of sports in HD, along with the usual compliment of young ladies tending bar and waiting tables.

"Hi, welcome to the Front Page my name is Missy," the cute young hostess said. "Will you be dining alone this evening?"

Maybe, maybe not.

"Just me," Ty said. "I'll sit at the bar if that's okay."

"Go right ahead," she ushered Ty that way with her hands toward the horseshoe shaped bar. Every stool had an occupant, except for one, located in between two ladies with their backs to each other.

He looked at the blonde one wearing an abundance of makeup. When she returned his look he asked, "Is this seat available?"

"Sure thing," she said, giving him a smile he's grown accustomed too.

"So," Ty asked. "What's good here? I'm starving."

"The beer." She smiled again, and he noticed her mug needed a refill.

"May I?" Ty asked.

"Sure," she said. "I'll be right back."

He watched with intent as she walked toward the restroom.

"What'll you have tonight, sport?" the bartender asked.

"Let's see, Simon," Ty replied reading the name on his tag. "A cheeseburger, fries, and two of whatever she's drinking," he said pointing to his new friend's empty glass.

Simon poured the two frosty beverages. He served them as she pulled herself back up to the bar. Ty raised his mug toward her.

"Salute!"

She returned the gesture.

"You're not from around here are you?"

"No, how rude of me. My name is Ty, pleasure to meet you."

"Maggie," she said with an inviting smile. "Nice to meet you. Thanks for the beer."

He nodded and winked his right eye.

★★★

"Thank God for technology," Chief Moore said as he and Hawkins entered onto Interstate 84. "Cell phone GPS locaters come in quite handy at times."

"Most people don't even know they exist," Hawkins replied.

"Well, I know of one person in particular, who'll be finding out about their usefulness in five minutes."

Hawkins turned away, looking out the passenger side window. Why did she ask me for coffee last week?

"Exit here Chief, that's it on the left."

They exited the Interstate and casually turned into the motel parking lot, stopping on the far side of the office. They both got out and gave the parking lot a visual inspection as they walked toward the entry, paying special attention the cars in front of the rooms. Hawkins knew the safest spot is always behind the Chief.

"Good evening sirs, do you have a reservation?"

"No, we're looking for someone we believe is staying here," Chief said as he and Hawkins displayed their badges. "A Jamaican guy, with long dread locks."

"Nobody like that stayed here, sorry."

Chief leaned over and grabbed the skinny clerk by the collar, "Look here punk. We know he was here earlier today. We traced his calls. You either tell me what room he's in or I'll throw your butt in jail. Now where is he?"

Trembling, the clerk answered, "Room 110, but he checked out a few minutes ago."

The Chief threw him back with just enough force to make him stumble. "Let me see your register."

"I can't do that sir, I'm sorry," he said, closing the book while backing away from the counter. "I can tell you he left with a white guy in a lime green Ford Taurus—a rental."

"You're not messing with me are you?"

"No, I'm not. I promise."

"How do you know it's a rental?"

"The Enterprise sticker on the back."

"Here's my card. If they come back you better call me. Understand?"

"Yes sir, thank you sir."

Hawkins followed Chief back outside staying well behind him.

"Son-of-a. . . " the Chief yelled. "Get in the car; let's grab a bite to eat before we head back to the city."

"I saw a sports bar a few exits back," Hawkins said. "Let's try that."

★★★

Having second thoughts about leaving Ty behind, Rasta headed back to find him. He'd spill his guts once they all got together. He exited the highway and made a u-turn under the overpass and headed back east to the strip center where he abandoned Ty. Hopefully he'd still be somewhere in the area.

He pulled his new rental car, a compact Nissan Versa, up to the red light. How do people drive these things? He reached below his seat to pull the lever again, hoping to gain more leg room. The seat slid back a few more notches, much better.

He adjusted the side view mirror and noticed a car approaching him from behind in the next lane over. He reached over to adjust the passenger side mirror. While he straightened himself up, he stole a glance at the car that pulled up next to him.

Oh my God!

He quickly made a right turn before the light turned green, hoping they didn't see him. As he drove off, he watched through the rearview to make sure they continued straight. Once they did, he whipped a u-turn and went after them.

What the hell are they doing here?

Rasta stayed safely behind the Chief's car not to be noticed. He followed them for two miles. They exited and pulled up into the strip center he left Ty at earlier today. They parked and entered the Front Page sports bar.

★★★

After Maggie and Ty drank a few beers, it was time to turn it up a notch.

"So Maggie, tell me, what do the locals do for fun 'round here?" Ty asked. "When they're not in this fabulous place."

Her look made him realize she was on to him, but she played along.

"Well, other than hanging around here, we go hiking, play with our dogs, and take long walks on the beach at sunset. We live in Utopia." She looked at him and laughed. "Actually we're a bunch of bored degenerates drinking our life away."

He leaned close to her and whispered, "It's an epidemic, but I know a remedy."

She leaned closer, and he could smell her perfume barely overpowering her beer breath. "Really? There's a remedy?"

"Yes there is. There's a remedy for everything."

She leaned closer.

"It goes like this," he started to whisper in her ear when he looked past her toward the front door.

"I'll be right back," he said. "Don't go anywhere."

He made his way around the opposite end of the bar toward the bathrooms as the hostess escorted the Chief and Hawkins to their table. Once they sat in their booth, he reversed course and headed toward the exit. He handed the other hostess standing by the door a $50 bill.

"An emergency just came up. This is for the young lady over there, thanks," he said, and slid out of the bar.

He quickly strode off toward the coffee shop with his head down hoping they didn't see him. That son of a bitch Rasta gave me up. He jumped off the curb and headed toward the street. He heard tires squealing as a red car jumped the curb and headed straight at him.

"Get in," Rasta shouted. "Hurry up."

Ty hesitated. "Why, so you can hold me while Moore and one of his goons come get me?"

"Get in or get caught, you have five seconds to decide."

He jumped in and they took off.

"Pull over behind the gas station," Ty said. "We need to talk."

Rasta drove past the station and headed eastbound.

"I said pull over, we need to get some things straight."

"Look man," Rasta said. "If I pull over, you're getting out and I'm not coming back for you. I suggest you shut up and let me drive."

"What's your game," Ty asked. "You leave me hanging, call Moore, and tell him where I am, then come back and get me? I don't get you."

"I had a change of heart, man, a change of heart, but I didn't call Moore."

Ty gave him the stare down, "Why should I believe you?"

"I don't care if you believe me. Do you want a ride or not?"

"Where we headed?"

"Back home. It's time to stop running, man," he said, "time to right a wrong."

He flipped Ty his cell, "Call Green and tell him we're on our way."

"Green? What happened to Boss Man?"

"Are you gonna call him or not?"

★★★

Reef finished telling me about his prior relationship with Barbara Lockwood, and now his rekindled relationship with Barbara Gillian, same woman, different last name.

"Does Ty know about this?" I asked Reef.

"Not that I'm aware of," he replied. "We were through when they met. Didn't see any reason to bring it up."

"I'm heading home," I told him. "I'll call you tomorrow. Do us both a favor. Stay away from the hooch, both of them." We both laughed, and I headed out of his office.

The clock on the dash showed 11 PM. Wow, what a day. My phone lit up and I saw restricted flash on the screen. The last time this happened my life took a downward spiral. I ignored it. A few seconds later the voicemail indicator sounded.

"Rich, answer your freaking phone."

My phone rang again, this time I answered it right away.

"Who's this?"

"Rich, it's me. I'm upstate with Rasta. We need to talk. We'll be at your apartment at 10 in the morning."

"You and Rasta?"

"Yes, I gotta go, see you tomorrow." End call.

It's late, but I need Reef and Hope here. "I know it's late, made contact with Ty and Rasta be at my apt 1000. Please confirm."

Wednesday, September 21, 2010 9:45 AM
Rectore Place, New York

"Let's hit the balcony while we wait on Reef and the others," I said handing a cup of coffee to Hope. She followed me outside. "They'll be here soon."

The crisp air and bright sun started its ascent over the horizon. The traffic on the river and esplanade are just getting started for the day. Soon both will be packed.

"It's beautiful out here," she said.

"Yes it is," I said. "Rosa and I've spent a lot of time here. We'd sit back listening to the music in the background and enjoy the sights."

"How's she doing?"

"She's struggling right now, there's complication with her pregnancy, but hopefully nothing serious. I love her. I love her, a lot. I'd rather be with her this morning than here, that's for sure."

There was an awkward silence.

"She seems like a wonderful woman," Hope said. "Hopefully when this is all done we can all become better acquainted. I think Rosa and I have a lot in common."

"Yeah well..." Reef buzzed the intercom letting me know he's in the lobby. I let him in and walked back to Hope. "Reef is here. I'm calling Rosa once this all settles down so we can get serious about getting back together."

"Rich, I'm not an expert on relationships, far from it, but don't put that off for this situation or any other issue that comes along. Show her you're serious. A woman needs a strong man in her life, especially when pregnant."

I looked at her. She's right. My life will never settle down long enough for it to be the right time. I need to make now the right time, and I will once we get through this Jack Harvey ordeal.

Reef knocked and I let him in.

"Hey Rich," Reef said and pointed, "Hope Brennan, I take it?"

"Yes, Reef, nice to meet you."

"Reef, grab a cup of coffee. We'll get started once the boys arrive." I waved Hope over from the balcony, and we sat around the table.

The intercom buzzed again, "Rich we're here let us up."

I got up, let them in the lobby, and waited by the door.

As Ty approached me, I grabbed his hand and pulled him close giving him a quick hug. I told Rasta to have a seat.

"Ty, this is my lawyer Hope Brennan. Hope this is Ty and Rasta, or AnDre St. Pierre?"

"Rasta's fine, thanks," he said smiling at me.

"Rasta, this is Reef Stantchin, my private investigator." They nodded at each other.

"I thought Mark would be here?" Ty asked. "Where's he?"

"Mark and I have parted ways," I said.

"Ty," Reef started. "You know we've been following you for the last four weeks or so, right?"

He nodded his head.

"Including the afternoon you went into Jack Harvey's apartment building. We also observed you exiting right before the police came, and then saw you jump into Rasta's cab."

"Hold on a second," I interrupted. "What were you doing in the area, Rasta?"

"Good question, Rich," Reef added.

We all looked at him for answers. He looked back at us and said, "I'll explain it all once Ty is done."

"I didn't kill Jack," Ty said. "He was dead when I arrived."

"Tell us step by step what happened," Reef asked.

"I knew Jack had been the one blackmailing me because I made up a few phony stories which only I could've told him. When these facts came out, it had to be him."

He took a long slow, deep breath. "So I decided to pay him a visit to tell him game's over. He can tell my wife everything. Hell, she already knew. Why should I continue paying him?" He looked at us for agreement, which we did. Reef squirmed in his seat.

"I knocked on his door and no one answered, but I knew he was there. And just like in the movies I shouted, open the door I know you're in there. Still nothing so I knocked harder, and the door opened. And I saw him on the floor. I went over to him, and without thinking, rolled him over, and there was a hunting knife and a puddle of blood. I scanned the room to see if he had anything of mine around. As I walked past the open door, a woman poked her head in. She saw the body, then me, and ran off. I split the scene."

"Did you see anyone leaving as you went in?" Hope asked.

"A tall, bald, strange sort of guy with a trench coat and a scar running down the length of his left cheek. He exited the elevator as I got in. We looked at each other, then he turned away real quick and headed off."

"I didn't see anyone exit before you did," Reef said.

Ty looked at him, "What are you trying to say?"

I put my hands up signaling time out before the argument started.

"Reef, do you still have those pictures of Mr. X?"

"At my office, why?"

"Didn't he have a scar?"

"I'll check when I get back. Continue Ty."

"I left the building freaked out. Then I heard the sirens and realized what just happened. Out of nowhere my personal savior, Rasta, pulled up and yelled for me to get in and get down. I did and heard the sirens approaching and then fade away."

We watched him take another long deep breath. "A few minutes later I heard him talking to you," Ty continued. "I asked him to drop me off at a deli around the corner, but he refused. We ended up on Long Island ditching the cab in a ravine. Rented a car and headed north. We were about to come back when we saw the news about you guys getting arrested, and warrants out for me."

"And Rasta just showed up out of the blue?"

"Yes. That thought never occurred to me until later," Ty said. "I'm just as curious as you are to hear his story."

"Did the lady get a good look at you?" Hope added. "Have you been to his place before?"

"I'm sure she did. I looked right at her, and yes I've been there a few times. I thought we were friends."

"That may hurt," Hope said. "We need to get you guys to a safe house."

"Hold on, Hope." I pointed at Rasta, "Your turn."

★★★

Rosa waited anxiously in the examination room. Being a doctor, she senses something's not right with her or the baby. Right now she needs comfort, a warm soothing touch letting her know it's okay. Rich is so immersed in his own issues, he wouldn't do much good. As hard as he's tried, she needed more than he could give right now. We'll have our time and it'll be sweet.

Looking around the room she grabbed a tabloid. Why do we subscribe to this garbage? She skimmed through the pages. The only thing she noticed was how fake everyone looked. She tossed it back on to the pile.

Her phone vibrated and Martha's name and number appeared.

"Hello," Rosa answered.

"Hi dear," Martha said. "It's been a while since we talked. How are you? How's Rich? Did Hope help you guys?"

"Yes she did. Rich hired her, and she's been a big help."

"Great, she's a blessing alright. How are you?"

"Well, for one thing, I'm pregnant. And Rich and I are planning to get back together once he gets out from under this case."

"That's wonderful! I'm so happy for you."

"It's funny you called," Rosa said. "I'm sitting here in my doctor's office waiting on the results of some tests, thinking I could really use someone to talk to. And, you called."

"You know dear, you're always on my mind, and in my prayers. What kind of tests are they running?"

"I gotta go, my doctor just came in. Are you free for lunch?"

"Yes, I am. Call me when you're done and we can meet up."

"I will," Rosa said. "And Martha..."

"Yes?"

"Thanks for always being there for me."

"You're welcome. We'll talk later, bye, bye."

★★★

"Where do I start?" Rasta said with a slight smile.

"How 'bout the beginning." I said without one.

"Six years ago I got in some trouble back in Jamaica. I fled to this country and started driving a cab to make money. Once things cooled down, I got a lawyer to help me straighten it all up."

"What kind of trouble?" Hope asked.

"What lawyer?" I asked.

"Your lawyer, and a bogus murder charge. So anyway, he said he'd take the case, but he'd need a favor in return."

What is he, the Godfather?

"I figure, sure whatever, man. No problem, just clear my name."

"Did he?" I asked.

"Not really, he just helped me change it to AnDre St. Pierre. He arranged everything from a new ID to a new social security number. I was happy, man. A new life."

I looked at the others. They leaned in toward the table waiting for the rest.

"Then the call came a year after we meet," he said pointing to me. "Rasta, this is Mark Stephens remember me? Well I'm calling in my favor. Meet me at my office tomorrow."

He looked around the table, and we all stared back at him.

"He told me I needed to work with him on a special project. If I didn't agree he'd let the authorities know my real identity. I'd get deported and face those charges. I wasn't going back so I played along. All I had to do was introduce you two. Once you," he said pointing to me, "and Stephens became partners, I'd be released."

"But they didn't let go, did they," Reef asked.

"Not even close," he replied. "The deeper it went, the deeper I got drug along. Always one more thing. I tell you man, I never expected it to get this way."

"So, the whole time you drove for me, you were passing on information to Stephens? Why?"

"Passing information, watching who you met with, and keeping tabs on you."

"Why?"

"You're a big shot Boss Man. For whatever reason he wanted to nail you, but you were clean. He had nothing on you."

I sat back in my chair, putting my hands behind my head. I still don't get it.

"Why was he after me?"

"I don't know why. I do know he was passing the info on to somebody else."

"Who." I asked.

"I don't know that either, but I do know he was indebted to someone like I was to him."

And.

"That's where Harvey came in," Rasta said.

"So your saying they arranged an informant to hand Rich insider information to build a case against him," Reef said.

"Bingo."

"So you guys were setting me up for the kill. All the while, Stephens had me believing everything we did was not illegal, maybe not entirely moral, but not illegal, even though it was."

"That's a good summary, Boss Man."

I got up and walked into the kitchen, trying to assimilate all he just said.

"Why did Harvey get involved?" I asked from the other room.

"He was indicted with securities fraud and hired Stephens as his lawyer," Rasta said.

"Who in turn convinced him to play along for immunity?" Hope chimed in.

"Apparently so, but he got greedy, and started blackmailing you for some reason," he said pointing to Ty.

"Then he tried to muscle his way in on you with his Mr. X thing. So they took him out."

Unbelievable, straight out of the movies.

"Who's they?" I asked.

"Other than Stephens and Harvey, I don't know."

"But whoever it is, now has Ty to thank for being at his apartment," Reef said.

"Then Rasta shows up and rescues him," Hope added, "which brings one more question. Why were you there at that exact moment?"

"This is where I get screwed," Rasta said. "I drive a guy over there who's supposed to shake Harvey up, ya know, hit him a few times, scare him a bit. I drop him off and make a circle around the block. I waited the 30 minutes as instructed. On my way to pick him up, I hear sirens buzzing all around and getting louder. I see Ty running from the building. I looked for Simon, but didn't see him. Instead of waiting around, I picked up Ty and we split. Then I learn I'm an accomplice to a murder. So we split the scene."

"The guy with the scar I saw in the elevator?" Ty asked.

"Goes by Scar Face, but yes," Rasta replied.

They all sat around the table quiet, while I stood in the kitchen entry behind them.

"Then we see the news about your arrest, and I decide to stay low for a while. But now, I'm ready to help you fight this," Rasta said.

"Why?" I asked him. "Why go through all this crap to frame me, and then decide to 'help' afterward?"

"I don't know," he said. "Call it a guilty conscious or whatever. All I can tell you is I'm willing to testify, or do whatever you need. I wanna go back home. I miss my family, and I need to get back there to clear my name. Time to stop running and right my wrongs."

"Reef, do you know any place they can go until I can figure out how to proceed with their defense?" Hope asked.

"I'll find something," he replied.

"They can stay here for the day," I added. "Where do we go from here?"

"I'm supposed to have coffee with Cody Hawkins," Hope said.

We all looked at her with surprise.

"We became close friends before I left the agency," she said. "Maybe he'll clue me in on a few details." She looked at her watch, "I'd better get going. I'll call you later, Rich."

"Now, what do we do with you two clowns?" I asked.

Wednesday, September 21, 2010 12:00 PM
Restaurant, New York

By the time Rosa reached the coffee shop, she'd cried every tear her body could produce. After she parked, she checked herself in the rearview mirror. What a mess! The small amount of make-up she wore had been smeared by her uncontrollable sobbing since leaving the doctor's office.

Gently, she swabbed the streaks with an applicator pad, hoping to reduce the damage from her weeping. Looking back at the mirror, she saw that her attempt did not work. She'd hit the restroom before Martha arrived, and get fixed there. She grabbed her purse and headed in.

"Over here dear," Martha flagged her down sitting back in the corner by the restrooms.

Great.

"Is everything okay, Rosa? You look like you've been crying?"

"Well, not really," she replied. "I'm having some major complications with the baby. It's really got me upset right now, sorry."

Martha came around to her side of the booth, and gave her a big hug.

"Do you want to talk about it?"

"I'll probably break down again, but yes I need to," Rosa replied. She felt her eyes tear up again. The flood will resume soon.

"My doctor said there's a chance one of us won't make it through the pregnancy. He suggested I terminate it."

"Oh, I'm so sorry. Did he say what the chances are?"

"What do you mean?"

"What are the odds?"

"Eighty percent." Rosa couldn't hold them back any further. The heavy sadness came upon her once again. "I don't know what to do?" she said, as the tears ran down her cheeks onto her shirt.

"Does Rich know?"

She shook her head, "He only knows about the complications we found last week. He's so caught up in that lawsuit I don't want to put any more stress on him."

Rosa looked up and saw a genuine look of compassion on Martha's face, unlike any of her other friends would ever produce. Another hug would be wonderful.

As if on cue, Martha came around from her side and hugged Rosa once again. Her hug allowed Martha to let go of herself. Her tears erupted into rivers causing Martha to cry as well.

"Let it out, dear," Martha said. "Let go of the pain if you can."

While they remained in each other's arms Martha started to pray.

"Dear heavenly Father, I ask you now to take your child and bless her beyond belief. Protect her and her unborn child. Perform a miracle in their life, Lord, I ask you to reach down right now, and soothe the pain and misery your child is feeling. I ask this in your mighty name!"

To her surprise, Rosa joined her with, "Amen."

"Thank you, Martha. I needed that more than you could ever imagine."

"You don't have to go through this alone, you know," Martha said.

"I know you'll be there for me. I appreciate it."

Martha looked at her with her warm smile. "I'll always be there for you, but I'm talking about God."

Rosa turned away.

"Please don't dismiss Him, Rosa. He's real, and He's calling upon you. He can provide the miracle you need. Why don't you lean on Him, and place all your burdens at the cross."

"I'm a doctor Martha. I know these types of illnesses can't be treated. Not with drugs, not with technology. How can God treat it?"

"That's a great question. I had a similar question six years ago when Robert died.

"I remember," Rosa said.

"Up until six months before his death, he lived a vibrant life," Martha continued.

Never smoked, hardly drank, worked out regularly, then all of sudden, out of nowhere, he gets lung cancer. I asked God, why him? What did he do to deserve this?"

Rosa looked intently into her eyes. She saw that pain still existed.

"The answer's quite simple. He didn't do anything to deserve it. Nobody does anything to deserve this. Nor does anybody do anything to deserve what you're facing. Our God is a God of love and mercy."

"Then why do these things happen?"

"Same question I asked. and I still ponder on it. The only answer I have is there are just some things which can't be explained away rationally It's all about faith."

"Faith in what?"

"Faith in the fact that God loves us and He'll provide for us in our time of joy and sorrow."

★★★

Hope and Hawkins decided to meet at a diner outside of Astoria. They found this place while working on a case several years ago. Although they never technically dated, she called it, "their place." She saw him in the corner looking toward the street. She stopped to watch him for a brief moment. He looked good, as always.

"Hey there," Hope yelled out.

He rose, while greeting her with his dazzling smile. "Good to see, Hope. I hear you've gotten yourself a big case."

Play it cool.

"Yeah, a long-time friend of the family referred me," she replied. "And you played a major role in the sting, didn't you?"

"Not really, Moore's in control--always. You know how he operates. I did pop the creepy lawyer though. It felt good nailing that perv."

Hope wanted to direct the conversation away from the case for now.

"So how've you been, outside of work? Any new flames?"

He made a slight hand movement as he glanced over the laminated menu laying on the table.

"Are you eating?" he asked her.

"The house salad, with balsamic vinaigrette. And you?"

"Not sure yet," he said, continuing to give the menu a stare down. "I think I've eaten everything they serve here at least twice. So, what's on your mind?"

"I was kind of hoping we could discuss the case, off the record, of course."

He looked at her with a smirk. "You know I can't do that. If Moore finds out he'll rip me apart."

He continued to review the menu as if something new would appear. He looked up and said, "I was sort of hoping you wanted to rekindle our friendship, not talk about work."

Now she really felt like a jerk.

"Sorry, I shouldn't have asked you that."

The waiter took the order, breaking the uncomfortable silence.

"What would you like to know?" He asked.

"Excuse me?"

"What do you want to know about the case?" he replied.

"Don't worry about It Cody. It's okay, we don't have to talk about it."

"I actually want to. There s a few things really bothering me about it."

"Such as?" Hope pressed him. If he's willing why not?

"Funny stuff," he replied. "I don't know exactly what; all I know is something's not right. I don't know Green, but I worked a minor case against him two years ago. We didn't find much, but Moore was so intert on bringing a charge. Then all of a sudden, just like that," he snapped his fingers, "Gone."

"Mark Stephens?"

"That's part of it," he responded. "When I did my own research into other cases against Green, I find three, with Stephens clearing them all up, except they never were truly cleared, just put away for a while."

"Are you aware of his background?"

"About his past indictments? Yes, also, about his propensity to beat women. I krow about that also."

"Come to think of it, I never saw him at the arraignment," Hope added.

"He never went to jail. He posted bail minutes after his arrest."

"Are you suggesting he's somehow hooked up with Moore?"

"It's possible--along with the cab driver. I'd like to talk with him, but we can't find him." We were close yesterday, but we missed him."

"You think the cabbie's involved as well?"

"Yes, he's mixed up in the whole thing as well."

"Well, I may be able to lead you to them," she boldly stated. "That is, if you're only wanting to talk. Otherwise, I've never seen them."

"Well, what are you waiting for?" He asked.

"There's something I need from you first."

"Well?"

"There is something you're not telling me Cody," Hope said. "There's more to this than your leading us to believe."

"How can you tell?"

"Your eyes, Cody. You don't look at me when you're talking, unless of course you're shy, which I know isn't the case. What is it?"

He shook his head, women, he thought.

"I can't divulge what is going on behind the scenes. What I can tell you is to keep your crew safe and away from the public. Trust me on this. We keep in touch. When the time is right you'll need to give them up."

"That's a big trust, Cody. How can I know you're not playing me?"

"You won't, but I ain't."

Wednesday, September 21, 2010 2:00 PM
Grocery Store, New York

Chief Moore stood in the long line waiting to check out from the corner grocery store. I hate this place. Can't these people move any faster? The woman in front of him pleading with her kids to keep quiet, nearly sent him over the edge.

"Give them a piece of gum or something," he told her. "Waiting in this line is bad enough without any screaming kids."

"Excuse me!" she looked dead in his eye with an angry, piercing stare. "Why don't you mind your own business?"

She turned her back to him and said, "It's okay kids, he's nothing but a miserable man, pay him no mind." She gathered them back into a group and moved up a notch in line. She turned back around, "Who do you think you are, anyway?"

"Excuse me ma'am," a gentler voice appeared from behind her and the kids. "Is everything okay?"

She turned around to a younger man wearing his "Hi, My Name Is Jimmy" manager's badge.

"This creep," she said pointing to Chief, "obviously needs patience."

Jimmy nodded and looked at Chief, "Sir, we are a bit shorthanded today,and we're doing everything we can to speed up the line. We'd all appreciate your cooperation."

While Jimmy spoke, the Chief's cell went off. With no regard, he raised his shoulder and pivoted away from Jimmy.

"Chief Moore," he answered loud enough for them to hear.

"Harry, have you made progress on apprehending the two suspects yet?" Pines asked.

"No sir, we haven't," he replied while walking away purposely leaving his cart in line.

"How can a cab driver and finance guy elude you for two weeks?" his voice increasing in volume and frustration.

"I thought you told me it's an airtight case. You don't even have the prime suspects in custody."

"I'm working on it, Bob. We're getting close."

"The only thing you're getting close too is out the door. Look Harry, we've been friends for many years, but your failure to finish cases is becoming an issue to me, and to Albany. I'll drop the charges on Green if you can't get this wrapped up soon."

"Don't do that to me Bob. I just need a little more time to put it all together." He saw Jimmy grab his cart out of the line pushing it away toward the back of the store.

"Wait," he shouted ripping the cart away from Jimmy's grasp trying to force his way in line. "I'm next."

"Sorry sir," Jimmy jumped in front of him saying,"You'll need to go to the end of the line."

"Get out of my way," Chief said, trying to force his way back into line. In the background he heard, "Harry, Harry, what in the world are you doing?" suddenly realizing he left his boss hanging on the line.

"Sorry, Bob," he said, but Pines already hung up. "Keep your stinking food." He pushed the cart toward Jimmy making his way toward the exit. The crowd broke out into a rousing applause mixed with unkind cheers and gestures as he left the store headed for his car.

His phone vibrated,   "Call me."

"What do you need?" Chief asked Hawkins approaching his car.

"I've got a solid lead on Gillian and St. Pierre," Hawkins replied.

"Where you at? I'll be right there."

"Before you get all excited, the only way for me to meet with them is alone. I'll fill you in after."

"I'm going with you Hawkins. This is my case."

"Sorry Chief, no disrespect, but it's me alone or no-body. I'll be in touch."

Hawkins hung up. Chief redialed him, but it went straight to voicemail.

"Don't go against me Hawk. Where are you?"

Instead of waiting on Hawkins, the Chief took a different angle.

★★★

I leaned against the railing of my balcony overlooking the mighty Hudson, lost in thought, when my cell vibrated, "Call me, luv u"

"Rosa, how's everything?" I asked. "How'd the appointment go?"

"We need to talk," she replied. "I know you're busy with the case and all..."

"When and where, Rosa? You're far more important than any case."

"I'll be at your place in an hour," she said. "My friend Martha will be coming along. Is that okay?"

"Yeah, I guess that'll be okay. Ty and Rasta are here until Reef finds them another place."

"Should we meet somewhere else then?"

"Absolutely not, this is your house too. I'll have Reef come by and get them. I'll see you soon, love you!"

"Okay, love you too."

I sensed the sadness in her voice; hopefully it's nothing real bad.

"Reef, come get them I have biz with Rosa to take care of"

Walking back into my crowded apartment symbolized just how much of a mess I'm in.

"Hey guys, help me clean up. Rosa's on her way over," I said. "Grab all your stuff from the second bedroom and get it ready. Reef is on his way over to get you."

"Do you think I should try to call Barbara again?" Ty asked.

"Not from here," I replied. "They probably have the lines tapped hoping you'll call."

Ty looked at me with wide eyes while he rubbed his thumb across his fingers rapidly.

"You called her from here, didn't you?" I raised my voice in unbelief.

He cleared his throat. Glancing away he said, "I didn't even think about them monitoring phone lines."

"You'd better start thinking about this whole mess Ty, or you're gonna get us all locked up. I can't believe you did that!"

"Sorry."

I shook my head mumbling some choice words loud enough for him to get the gist.

"Rasta, give me your phone," I commanded. "Where's the settings button?"

"We already disabled the GPS locator," he said.

"Who did it, you or Ty?" I asked. Rasta pointed to Ty.

Let's make sure he did it right. I scrolled through the cheap phone looking for settings features.

"It's still on! What the..." I looked at Ty holding out my hands in disbelief. "Dude! Get your head in the game."

After disabling the device, I called Reef.

"I'm right around the corner," he said. "Tell them to meet me at the roundabout on South End in two minutes. And be discreet." End call.

"Get your stuff and use the elevator on the other side of the hall, not the one you came up on. This will bring you down to the parking garage. Go down one flight of stairs. Exit through the second exit door. Follow the sidewalk past the hair cutting place. You'll come to Thames Street. Go left to South End, go right till you hit the Roundabout. There's a park with benches. Wait there for Reef. See you guys later."

As they walked down the hall I yelled to them, "Ty." He turned around. I pointed to my right temple, "Head in the game. We're counting on you." He nodded and took off to catch up with Rasta.

I put the kettle on the stove, preparing water for Rosa's tea while straightening up the kitchen and living room. There's something missing. The intercom buzzed, forcing me out of my trance.

"It's me, Rosa."

"Come on up baby, door's open," I said, walking back to the kitchen to fix the tea for Rosa and Martha. I cracked open a beer for myself. The gentle knock informed me they arrived. As they entered, Rosa's puffed eyes indicated she'd been crying for quite a while. I greeted her with a tight hug and kiss on the neck. She held me tight in return. I felt her tremble in my arms.

"It's okay baby," I whispered into her ear. "Whatever's wrong we'll deal with it together."

"I know," she said, and released her arms from my waist. "Rich, you remember Martha?"

"Of course, good to see you again."

She gave me a quick hug, "Nice to see you too."

"I made you two some tea. How do you take yours, Martha?"

"Cream and sugar's fine, thanks."

I walked them toward the couch, then headed back to the kitchen to fetch the tea, and my beer.

Placing their cups on the coffee table, I sat down next to Rosa. Martha sat across from us on the recliner.

"Very nice place you have, Rich," Martha said breaking the silence. "A wonderful view as well."

"Thanks," I said. "Got a great deal on it. Once this is over, I'll be selling it so we can get a place more family oriented." I saw Rosa try to smile. She's hurting.

"There's a major complication with the baby," Rosa opened up with. "I have what's known as Pre-eclampsia. Not too bad in itself, but mine is a rare strain, placing both of us at high risk. The doctor suggests I terminate it, but I could never do that."

"I'm not at all familiar with what you're saying, what is pre-eclampsia? By the word, is there an eclampsia also?"

"Yes, pre can turn into the full-blown disease. The short of it is, eclampsia causes seizures, and a host of other conditions that can kill me and the baby."

I looked at Martha, then back at Rosa, and took a drink of my beer, hoping to relieve my hurt deep inside, which I knew it wouldn't.

"Is it treatable? I mean, can't we do something to minimize the effects?"

"The only thing they can do is monitor it. There are some treatments for the typical strain, but not mine."

I looked again at Martha while she fidgeted in her chair. My look invited her into the conversation.

"May I," she asked anyway. Our history hasn't been real kind.

"Sure, Martha, please," I replied.

"There are many ways to look at this," she started. "The one I'd use, of course, is God's view, but that's me, and my views aren't the same as yours."

She looked at me. I nodded for her to continue. The few times we talked God always came up. I shut her down the last time. Looking back, much harder than I should have.

"Terminating the pregnancy due to personal reasons is purely wrong. When it's due to medical reasons, there's some leeway, but there'll always be regret. My thoughts on the way here is you'll both be faced with decisions only you two can make. Outsiders, including me can give you advice, but you two will have to bear the full burden of a decision that no one should have to make."

She started to tear up. My respect for her just grew monumentally. No preaching, just solid advice. Rosa leaned toward me with open arms. I accepted her invitation and embraced her.

A sound from the hallway caught my attention. As I turned to look, the front door burst open, followed by a swarm of police officers--pistols pointed directly at us.

"Hands on your heads, all of you, right now!"

The three of us sat there with our hands behind our heads. I looked at Rosa. Her eyes wide open in panic. I looked at Martha. Her eyes closed whispering something. Is she praying?

I looked toward the door as the officers parted. Through the opening, Chief Moore came striding in like an emperor entering a ballroom.

"Where are they?" he asked.

"Where's who?" I replied.

"Your two accomplices," he said, pointing to Rosa and Martha. "Are these them?"

"What are you talking about? And do you have any warrants to come busting through my door?"

"I don't need any stinking warrant Green. You're a criminal. Now where are they?"

"Who?"

"Gillian and St. Pierre. Don't play dumb, where are they?" He motioned for the officers to start searching my apartment.

"Hold on," I said loudly. "Where's your search warrant?"

"Don't mind him, search the place," he commanded. "The three of you; in the hallway."

They looked at me. I shook my head.

"Now, " he yelled, "or I'll move you myself."

They looked back at me, and this time I nodded. "Let's go," I said softly.

Chief Moore followed us into the hallway.

"You'd better have a good reason for this," I told him. "You do realize Pines and I go way back."

"Your money and friendship won't help you this time, Green. You'll be going away for a long time."

"We'll see about that."

"Faces against the wall," Chief said. "Frisk them thoroughly, he instructed the officers stationed outside the apartment."

"Hands out in front touching the wall," one of them shouted.

While they patted me down, the lead officer emerged from inside. He whispered into Moore's ear.

"Check again," Moore said.

The officer responded, "There's nothing," with his hands in front of him.

I'm going to strangle Ty.

Moore walked up behind me, almost touching me with his entire body."I know they were here, Green. You'll make one too many mistakes, and I'll be there to nail you!"

He turned back to the lead officer, "Get your men and let's go." He turned back to me, "Watch your ass, Green!" They marched out of my apartment one by one, giving us their best mean looks. Some worked.

After the final one walked past, I gently put my hand on Rosa's shoulder and guided her back into my apartment. I felt violated, our personal space invaded.

"You going to let them get away with this?" Rosa asked.

"I'm more concerned about you two right now."

"Don't worry about us, Rich," Rosa responded. "Call Hope and get her on that guys butt."

"I'm okay as well," Martha said. "Startled and scared, but okay. I should probably get going."

"I'll be back later, Rich," Rosa said. "I need to take her back home."

We hugged and kissed each other lightly. I didn't want to let her go.

"How about I go with you two?"

"Really?" Rosa asked. "What about your restrictions?"

"I don't care. Come on, let's go."

"Before we go, I have a question for you, Martha." I had to ask. "Right before we went to the hall, you had your eyes closed saying something."

"I prayed, Rich," she replied. "I prayed for our safety and God's protection."

"It seems to have worked."

"It always does."

Wednesday, September 21, 2010 4:30 PM
Safe House, New Jersey

Reef grabbed a garage door opener from the console and drove Ty and St. Pierre into the garage of his deceased grandparents' house. He inherited the 4700 square foot rancher three years ago, using it only when he needed to get away or times like this. Sitting less than one-half mile off Interstate 78, it's impossible to see from the highway because of the heavily wooded hills surrounding the two acre tract. The secluded location adds an extra level of privacy, which comes in handy for both occasions.

"You guys take the bedrooms upstairs," Reef said. "Keep the blinds closed at all times. No phone calls, period!"

He looked at Ty, "Got it?"

"Yeah, I got it," Ty replied. "No phone calls and keep the blinds closed at all times."

"My parents didn't have a racial bone in their body, but the community may find it odd that a black man with dreadlocks is suddenly in my parents' house."

St. Pierre looked at Reef, "Just telling you how it is. No need to draw unwanted attention this way. Stay inside."

"What about the television?" Ty asked.

"It has every channel known to man," Reef replied. "Let's take a food inventory. You'll be here for several days so we need to make sure there's plenty to eat. Because once I leave, you're on your own, and you can't leave the house for any reason."

"Got it, man," St. Pierre said.

"Ty?"

"Yes, Reef. I got it, already told you."

"Do I call you Rasta, or what?" Reef asked him.

"Rasta is fine," he replied.

"Okay, Rasta. Do you know anything about Scarface? Name? Alias? Who hired him? Anything we can trace?"

"He's hooked up in some way to Stephens, I think," he replied. "I only saw him once before."

"Where?"

"Leaving Stephens office one day."

"You sure that's all you know?"

They listed the items Reef should pick up from the local grocery store. He reiterated the need to keep the blinds shut and staying indoors at all times, and he left.

On the way he called Stan the man. He answered on the first ring.

"Reef! What or who can I help you find?"

"We're looking for a thug called Scarface. A former client of Mark Stephens."

"Scarface? Really?"

"What can I say, that's what they call him."

"I may need a little more info than that. I'm good, but not that good."

"You'll be receiving a fed-ex in the morning with some pictures of him. Will that help?"

★★★

"Martha, go ahead and sit up front," I said. "I'm fine in the back."

As Rosa pulled out of the parking garage on to Rectore, I noticed a dark black Crown Victoria pull away from the curb behind us.

I leaned in between the two from seats to get a glimpse of the gas gauge. "Looks like you should stop for gas," I said. "Go by the Shell Station down by the park."

"I'll be fine,"

"Just go by the Shell station. Trust me on this."

The station is on a one way street requiring quite a few turns to get there. Taking this route will confirm if we're being followed, or if I'm just paranoid.

Rosa pulled in to the station, and I jumped out trying not to look directly at the car approaching. The driver slowed as the car passed. Through the corner of my eye I saw a white male with aviator sunglasses staring in our direction. He proceeded two blocks, turning left at the stop sign. I finished pumping the gas, walked around to Rosa's window, and waved for her to exit.

She got out and shut the door, "We're being followed," I told her. "It'll be best if I stay behind. No need to get us all in trouble by leaving Manhattan. I'll walk back to my place."

She looked around for the car. I pulled her close and hugged her with a strong embrace.

"He turned at that stop sign up ahead. He's probably waiting around the corner."

"You think it's safe to walk back?"

"It may be better if your drop me off in front of my apartment."

I walked back around the rear of her SUV and got back in. Rosa drove by the stop sign up ahead. Sure enough the black car pulled in behind us.

"Did you see the car that just pulled behind us?"

She nodded in the rearview.

"That's him," I said. "Pull up to the front of my building so he can see me get out. Then wait until I come back to the car before you leave."

"What are you going to do?"

"Find out who it is, baby."

We pulled up in front and she parked in one of the residence spots on the street. I jumped up and jogged toward the lobby, watching for the car. I saw him park at the corner of South End and Rectore.

I took the same route Ty and Rasta used to escape earlier putting me one block behind my follower. Crossing to the other side of South End, and blending in with the crowd, I'd be able to approach him without being seen. When I got two cars behind, I darted out into the street and ran up to his window grabbing the door handle before he could lock the door.

I startled him, and he reached to his side where I saw his holster and I immediately backed off while raising my arms.

"You won't need that Mister," I said. "Why are you following me?"

He closed the door and took off without saying a word. I walked around the corner up to Rosa's SUV and knocked on the window.

"It's a cop." I explained to Rosa and Martha. "You guys should get going. Sorry for all the trouble I'm causing."

"I'll call you later so we can talk about the baby," Rosa replied.

I gave her a kiss and waved bye to Martha as they took off.

My phone buzzed with a call from Reef.

"Rich, I got a great idea," Reef started. "Let's get with Stephens to compare notes on the case. See what he's willing to share."

"We can quiz him about his connections with Moore, and St.Pierre," I responded tracking along with him.

"I'm thinking more about that Scarface character. If we can get any kind of information about him, Stan the man can do what he does best."

"Good plan. I'll call you back."

I hung up and dialed Stephens. He answered on the third ring.

"Rich, what's good?" he asked.

"Let's get together tomorrow," I said. "We can compare notes, making sure our cases are in synch."

I heard some scuttling of feet and giggling in the background. Some things never change.

"Can I call you back tomorrow," he replied. "I'm kind of busy right now."

"Better yet, we'll be at the dump at nine-thirty. See you then." End call.

"Reef, meet at dump 0930."

Thursday September 22, 2010 09:00 AM
IPB Office, New York

Hawkins walked softly toward Chief Moore's office door, and knocked three times rapidly. Before Moore could answer, "Chief, it's Hawkins. May I come in?"

He heard a mumbled response so he entered.

"I'm sure by now you've heard about the raid on Green's apartment yesterday," Chief started.

"Yes I did," Hawkins replied. "It's all over the street. With all due respect, I told you I have a strong lead on their location."

"We're a team Hawk. You can't keep secrets from me. What you know, I must know. Now where are they?"

"Good question. And one I don't have the answer too," Hawkins replied. "Not only did you scare them off, but you damaged my credibility with my connection."

"If you'd told me yesterday, I'd grabbed them, and we wouldn't be having this conversation."

"That's just it. I didn't know yesterday. I only had a strong lead, which is now broken. We're back to square one."

"So Hawk, I heard you and Brennan have been meeting?"

"Steele's been following me again? Seems like an awful waste of agency funds, don't you think? You must have better things for him to do--maybe, catch some criminals?"

"I'm leery of you when it comes to her," he said raising his right eyebrow. "You two created a strong friendship before she left. I don't think I need to tell you the ramifications of associating with her again, do I?"

"First, we met at her request. I thought it may do some good to see what she knows. Which, by the way, is nothing. Second, neither you nor anyone else determines who I see or hang out with. You're my boss Chief, not my father. If there's nothing else, I have paperwork to finish."

Hawkins got up to leave the office. "One more thing Chief. There's talk about a thug known as Scarface? An eye witness can place him at Harvey's place prior to Gillian. Just thought you should know."

Chief closed his eyes and clenched his lips together. He forced a fake smile, "Thanks, Hawk, I'll look into it."

★★★

Reef and I went over our strategy from last night. Our goal is to find out how deep Stephens is connected to this case. We all believe he's much more than a defendant. We also ran this by Hope to make sure we aren't risking anything she's working on.

"Our best offense is a good defense," she told us. "We can't let on that we know anything about his prior dealings with Moore, and St. Pierre." She cautioned us about asking too many pointed questions. It'll be best if we lead him toward the answers we seek, instead of outright asking.

My cab dropped me off in front of the nasty dry cleaners below the dump. I looked up at the second story windows. Seeing the dirt and grime from this view amused me for a second. Then reality set in. How did I allow this to get so far out of hand?

I entered the steamy building, climbing up the worn stairs for the last time, hopefully. Not much has changed since my last visit, except all the trinkets and pictures cluttering Shelley's desk are gone.

"Back here Rich," Stephens called to me from his office. "We're back here."

I poked my head in spotting Stephens and his lawyer, Robert Sawyer. Bookends.

"Rich..." Sawyer stood up and offered his hand. "I hear you're engaged with a child on the way. How'd you manage that?"

"Have you heard from Reef?" I asked Stephens, discounting Sawyer and his comment completely.

"No, I figured you'd come together," he replied. "What have you found out?"

"We'll wait on Reef," I responded. I walked to the window looking down to the street replaying the scene with Rasta and Cromack. I knew something was up with them. As much as a sleaze that Stephens is, it's still hard to believe he's working for the feds.

"Here he comes," I said, walking away from the window and taking the seat adjacent from Stephens. Once Reef entered the room we got started.

"I ended up hiring Hope Brennan after all," I started the conversation with a neutral statement as an ice breaker. "She worked for the IPB before becoming an attorney."

"So she's in good with Moore and his agents?" Stephens asked. "That can be beneficial."

"No, she's not in good with them anymore, and she doesn't need to be. She's sharp, and she has an assistant who can find out anything about anybody." I winced. Slow down you're leading them down the wrong path.

"Like what?" Sawyer budded in.

"Like stuff," I replied. "What have you found out about Ty and Rasta?"

"They'll still at large," Sawyer said. "Both are connected to the Harvey murder with good reason."

"Why's that?" Reef asked.

"Eye witness and motive. The two main things cop's need to bring a case."

"They aren't the only ones with motive," I added. "Word has it Harvey played a few others as well."

Stephens started to scratch the back of his head. "Where'd you hear that?"

"Are you telling me you haven't heard that?" I asked him. He shook his head as did Sawyer. "Come on, now. You're both lawyers. You didn't think to check who Harvey dealt with in the past?" I shook my head and puckered my lips, "Wow. Good thing I hired Brennan."

"It don't matter who Harvey dealt with, Rich," Stephens said. "Everybody knows Ty did it, and hired your cabbie for the get-a-way car."

"It looked like that at first," Reef said nodding his head.

"What do you mean at first?"

"At first, all the evidence pointed to Ty, until the eyewitness told police she saw another man leaving Harvey's place before Ty even got there. You didn't know this either?"

"Some Scarface character," Reef continued. "We believe our guys uncovered his identity last night. That's awesome right?"

They both tried to act cool, as if no big deal. Reef and I knew better.

"A thug calling himself Scarface?" Stephens mumbled. "What do you know about him?"

"Not a lot, yet," I said. "We just found out about him. But we have a strong lead on who he is and who he's working for. We'll have it pinned down by tomorrow."

Stephens started to fidget. I saw a few drops of sweat appear along his hairline.

"Keep us posted, will ya," Sawyer asked.

"Of course," I lied to him. "What about you two? Surely, you've uncovered something proving our innocence, haven't you?"

"Actually we've been spending our time defending me," Stephens replied. "Ty can worry about himself."

"You and I are in this together, Mark," I said, "Ty's part of our business."

"We motioned to be tried separately, Rich," Sawyer said. "We don't stand a chance in hell if we stick together."

I felt my anger start to rise.

"You don't stand a chance period," I said as I stood up and headed out of the stuffy room. Reef followed me out.

"Watch yourself, Rich," Stephens yelled. "You don't know who you're dealing with over there. They're serious."

I walked back to the door and stuck my head in, "You better watch yourself, little man. I may surprise you."

Friday September 30, 2010 3:00 PM
Safe House, New Jersey

Reef and I planned to spend the weekend in Jersey, keeping our two inmates in check. Rosa's mother is in town keeping her busy the entire weekend.

I called Ty on our pre-paid cells, which can't be traced. "We're on our way," I said.

"Hurry," he replied. "We're nearly out of everything."

"We'll be there in an hour and a half. Can you wait that long?"

"I can order a pizza in the meantime."

"Bad idea, Ty. You're in hiding, remember? We'll see you in a few." End call.

Reef looked over to me from the divers seat. He loves to drive, especially my STS.

"What did he say about pizza?" he asked.

"He wanted to order a pizza before we got there. Sometimes I wonder about his reasoning."

"Put yourself in his place," Reef stated, "wanted for murder, cooped up with 'Boss Man' for weeks, and his marriage on the rocks. He's probably not thinking real clear."

He had a point, except Ty's lack of common sense is not a new phenomenon.

Better to change the subject. First text Rosa. "Hi love, nearly there tell mom I said Hi. C u sunday. Luv u!"

"You like this car, don't you?" I asked Reef an obvious question. "I'll make you a sweet deal on it once this is all done. I may even throw the Carrera in as a bonus."

"I'm sure you will," he replied. "By the time this is all done, you may have to give me both cars, plus cash to settle up."

"Nice!" I said. "You do take payments, right?"

"Only from trustworthy individuals who aren't running from the law."

"Ya know any of them?"

He turned toward again, "very few." We both laughed.

As we drove, I adjusted my seat back and closed my eyes.

Four years ago I wanted to be the most feared man on the Street. Now, I'm the most embarrassed, broken man on the Street. We're sheltering two alleged murderers. One of whom is a Jamaican dude who betrayed me. I hired a Christian lawyer with a nerdy assistant who hates his name. And to top it all off, my pregnant fiancé and I will have to decide whose life to spare--hers or the baby's. My phone vibrated breaking my trance. "Hey baby, she said hi, going to store. stay safe, love you."

"Reef, stop by the store before we get to the house," I said. "Let's pick up a few beers, and try to relax and have some fun tonight."

"Add a glass or two of Glenlivet as a night cap," he said. "Sure."

We arrived at the safe house finding it still in one piece without any damage. We entered through the unlocked interior garage door. We heard Ty and St. Pierre arguing about which letter the Wheel of Fortune contestant should pick.

"Could be worse," I whispered to Reef.

Reef raised his finger to his mouth and gently walked in behind them, "Freeze," he yelled. "Police, hands in the air!"

They jumped up and danced around in a panic. Reef and I busted up laughing.

"What the heck?" Ty yelled. "You almost gave me a heart attack."

"You guys need to practice a bit more security," Reef said. "You left the garage wide open. The cops could've walked right in and had you before you knew what happened."

"You could get yourself shot doing that, man," St. Pierre added.

"Shut-up and help grab the groceries out of the car," I told him. "Do you even have a gun?"

"That's not the point, man."

"We bought some drinks, and a deck of cards," I said. "Time to play some serious poker. I need some cash."

"What kind of drinks," Ty asked.

"A case of Dos Equis for you and Rich, a twelve pack of Red Stripe for St. Pierre, and a bottle of Glenlivet for me," Reef said.

"Just cause I'm Jamaican you think I drink Red Stripe?"

"No, just thought I'd throw that in to see if you were listening. Relax, man," Reef replied.

I walked out to my car and closed the garage door calling for the others to help unload our weekend supplies.

"Once we get this stuff put up, we can get down to business," I said. "Reef, it's time."

"For what?" he yelled back.

"Time to quench my thirst;' I replied yelling back, "pour me a Dos Equis."

"I guess I'll take a Red Stripe," St. Pierre chimed in. "It'll keep me oppressed."

We all laughed. "How about we un-oppress you, but take all your money playing cards?"

"Won't take long, man," he said. "It's not like I have a job or anything. I gave that up helping this clown escape. Remember?"

"What I remember is you spying on me to get my butt tossed in the clink," I said. "That's what I remember."

"Yes, but I repented, man. I'm on your side now."

"Well, I can sleep better knowing you're on my side now."

"Kiss and make up, so we can deal the cards," Reef said. "You two aren't going be argue all weekend are you?"

"If you don't behave, you'll be sent to your rooms without any beer," Ty added. "Got it?"

"Yes dad," we said in unison.

"Now, one of you get me a beer, the other can deal the cards," Ty said snapping his fingers. "Let's go, dealer's choice."

We played cards through most of the evening, taking a break only to order and devour four large pizzas from the Italian place down the road. Ty, as we expected, fell in love with the delivery girl. His lust is out of control.

By the time we called it quits for the evening, I felt good about our relationships, especially with St. Pierre, who will now be known as Dre. He may hold the trump card we need to clear our names.

Before passing out for the night, I shot Rosa an "I love you" text.

Saturday January 28, 2012 10:00 AM
Safe House, NJ

I awoke the next morning at 10 AM to a vibrating phone and a massive headache. I reached down to my phone and saw a few missed calls, a voice mail, and a text from Rosa. "Good Night, Love you too, call me in the AM"

The missed calls came from Hope and Stanley. I played the voicemail. After hearing it called Hope.

"Did you get my message?" Hope asked.

"Yes, I did. Are you sure that's a good idea? Can you trust him?"

"Absolutely. What did you get out of Stephens the other day?"

"He's hiding something, but he didn't really divulge anything we didn't already know."

"Well, Stan has found the Scarface character."

"Are you serious? How?"

"He's awesome, that's how."

"Obviously, but how?"

"He found a clipping from the Daily News describing a guy who used the same name. It became quite popular in the mid-80's after Pacino's movie. We found out where he lives, and showed his picture to a police contact who confirmed it's the same guy the witness saw."

"Have you talked with him yet?"

"No. No way. I don't want to scare him off, so we sent our new ally. The same guy who's going to help us put this to rest."

"About using him, are you sure?"

"Sure as Jesus is my Savior."

"That's as sure as it gets, I guess. We're in Jersey at the safe house. I'll get with Reef later today and call you. Tell Stanley he's a genius."

Before going out to the kitchen to get in on the wonderful breakfast I smell, I called Rosa.

"Good Morning Sweetie," I said, once she answered. "I have a bit of a hangover this morning. Just now getting my butt out of bed."

"Serves you right. What do you have planned for today? Mom and I are going to visit some old friends then pick up Martha this evening."

"Sounds like fun. We're not going to do much of anything other than clean-up the house, and help Reef with yard work. This evening, I plan on winning back the $20 Dre won last night."

"Dre?"

"Rasta's new name, short for Andrew."

"Got you. I'll call you later this afternoon. Behave yourself."

"Love you, have fun with mom," I replied and hung up.

★★★

Listening to the tick, tock, tick, tock of the huge grandfather clock in the corner helped me relax. Watching the golden, sword-shaped pendulum swing back and forth knocked me out. The 8 PM gong scared the life out of me, causing me to nearly fall off the sofa. I wiped my eyes walking to the bathroom, stubbing my toe on the corner of Dre's head.

"What the heck, man," he rolled over grabbing the side of his face. "You almost poked my eye out."

"Sorry, I didn't see you."

Reef and Ty cracked up, making fun of his awkward sounding outburst. They jawed at each other before I put a stop to it.

"I'm going stir crazy in here man," Dre said. "Can we take a drive or something? I need sunshine and fresh air."

"What do you think?" I asked Reef.

"Why not."

We piled into the Caddy, and took off with Reef at the controls. I made Ty and Dre wear baseball hats pulled down to the bridge of their noses. Even though the area isn't crowded, you can't take chances.

"Where would you two like to go?"

"As bad as this sounds I'm craving a MacDonald's hamburger," Ty said, "and a shake."

"Of all the things we could do, man, and you ask for MacDonald's?" Dre paused then said, "You buying, right man?"

I sighed. They're both a piece of work.

New Jersey is quite a beautiful state. Once you get west of Newark, that is. The drive from Blaise's parents to the nearest MacDonald's takes us through the rolling hills and thick forest bordering both sides of the winding two lane state road. Every half-mile or so as you negotiate one of the sharp curves. Another secluded home site sits back off the road on the inside of the curve. This prevents head-lights from oncoming cars to shine into the windows of the enormous homes. The layout of the neighborhood is well thought out.

He slowed down to make a sharp left as we passed a humungous house. All of us stared at the monstrosity of a structure. I've seen big houses in my day; this one rivals all of them. Must be 10,000 square feet at least.

"That's the Montgomery Estate," Reef said. "Old oil money built that kingdom. Went to private school with one of the boys." Reef eased off the accelerator pedal, giving us the opportunity to gawk at the estate some more.

Elm street dead ends into Main Street. Once the light turned green Reef hung a left. We made a few more turns bringing us back into civilization.

"See that church over there," Reef pointed to his left. "I used to be the pastor."

"Yeah, right," I replied. "I used to be President of the United States, but it didn't pay enough so I changed my career to master of insider trading and fugitive hider."

My backseat fan club cracked up.

"It's true," he said. "Remember our conversation a few weeks ago about God and his connection to our lives?"

I nodded.

"Well, God is connected to our lives so many ways it'll blow your mind. Even if you're not a believer."

"What happened? How on earth did you get from Pastor to Private Investigator? Seems like polar opposites."

"Not as much as you'd think. Both roles help people get out of jams. They hit it from differing perspectives."

"So why did you quit the church gig?" I asked him.

"It's not a long story, but you may not understand the reason."

"Try me."

"I lost my faith. I poured my life into that church, giving up my personal life to grow the small membership into a thriving body of Christ. To outsiders and most of the congregation, I had it made. They never experienced the backstabbing, infighting, and power struggles that developed over time."

Reef slowed down approaching a stop sign. He rolled through it without stopping.

"It all came to a head one day when--oh great!"

"What?" I asked.

He made a fist and pointed behind us with his thumb.

The red and blue lights illuminated the inside of my car.

"What the heck?" Reef said.

"You ran the stop sign, man."

He pulled over and waited for the officer to exit his cruiser. I opened the glove box to get my insurance card and registration. When I pulled them out, several unpaid parking tickets fell to the floor. I brushed them under the seat and turned around.

"You guys act like normal people. Better yet, don't say a word."

The officer flicked on his spotlight aiming it at the rear-view mirror blinding all of us. Reef rolled down the window in anticipation of his visit.

"Good evening sir," the officer said. "In a hurry?"

He didn't look one day over 18. Must be a rookie.

"No officer, I'm not."

"Do you know why I pulled you over?"

"I didn't stop at the stop sign back there?"

"Yes." He pointed his flashlight at each of us, staring us down.

"You guys from New York?"

"Yes, but I grew up on Elm Street. We're spending the weekend at my parents' old house. You know, get away from the big city for a few days."

"Where are you headed now?"

"MacDonald's to get a quick bite." Reef handed him his license and the other documents before he asked for them. He shined his light at the cards.

"Good thing they have a dollar menu. Wanna know why?"

"Why's that officer?" Reef replied. He turned to me arching his right eyebrow.

"That's all you can afford after this ticket." He laughed to himself. "Damn city boys think they can break all the rules," he said under his breath, but loud enough for us to hear. "Which one of you is the owner of the vehicle?"

"I am, officer."

"Let me see your license. Are these your girlfriends... in the back?"

"Just friends of ours," Reef replied.

Rookie studied my license for a few seconds. Then shined his light in my eyes causing me to squint and see blue spots.

"I'll be right back." He took our licenses back to the cruiser. I adjusted the rearview to follow his movements.

"I'm screwed. Unpaid tickets, and I'm not supposed to be off the island."

"Hold tight, Rich. New Jersey doesn't always check out of state records."

Halfway back he spoke into the mic clipped to his collar. Then he performed a perfect about-face that his commander would be proud of. The sweat started forming on my brow. I could see the nosey passengers in the oncoming vehicles stare into my car. I'm sure I do the same thing.

"I need both of you to step out of the car and stand over there by the street sign. You two in the back, give me your driver's license and sit right there. Don't move."

We got out and marched over to the sign as instructed. He snatched their licenses and moved to the back of my car. Another siren off in the distance increased in volume. Reef and I looked at each other.

"Now we're all screwed," I whispered to him.

The second squad car whipped in to the opening behind my car. A large man got out. He pulled up his pants trying to cover his over-stuffed belly. He probably brags about still wearing a size 32 after all these years. The "rookie" handed our licenses to "big boy" amongst flailing arms and pointing. His excitement level is hard to miss, must be his first bust.

Big boy motioned for him to calm down, he pointed back and forth between the two of them saying something.

"Good cop, bad cop?" I whispered to Reef.

"Reef Stantchin from Elm Street and Richard Green from Wall Street?" Big boy asked.

We nodded.

"And the two clowns in the back, anyone I should be aware of?"

"No sir," I replied. "Just two of our friends from back home."

He starred us down for what seemed an eternity.

"Reef, did you ever attend John F Kennedy High School?"

"No, I went to First Community Academy."

He looked at Reef with a devious grin.

"Green, did you know you have seven parking tickets outstanding in New York?"

"Yes officer, I did." My underarm perspiration started to soak through my shirt. I'll take the dive in hopes he doesn't check on Ty and Dre.

"I intended to pay them, but I forgot."

"Forgetting one, I can deal with. But seven?" Big Boy shook his head like a disappointed father to his troubled son. "Stantchin? Does the name Larry Wilber ring a bell?"

He grabbed his chin, "Larry Wilber?" He paced a few steps. "The Larry Wilber who lived three houses down from Mary Stone on Maple Drive?"

"Yes, the one you always beat up as a kid." We all smiled. He pointed to his badge. "The same one," he said. Our smiles ended.

"Didn't you Pastor a church for a while?" Larry asked.

"Yes, I married you and Mary there."

"Yes you did. Small world, isn't it?"

"How's Mary doing? I haven t seen her in years."

"She's dead, but thanks for asking."

Reef pursed his lips emitting a silent, o-kayyyy.

"I can nail you two, especially you, big shot," he said pointing at me. "But I won t--this time. But we'll be watching you two closely. If I see you're up to something, I'll bust the two of you good. Now get in your car and get the hell out of here."

He threw the licenses at us and stood there with his hands on his hips. Neither of us moved.

"Well?" rookie said. "Grab your stuff and scram."

We snatched the licenses from the street, jumped in the car, and took off.

"I think we'll pass on MacDonald's tonight," I said once back in the car.

"Everybody pack their stuff, we need to get out of here," I said once we pulled into the garage.

"Make the house look like it did before we got here," Reef added. "This way, if the police come calling, they won't suspect anything."

Sunday, January 29, 2012 06:30 AM

I awoke once again to my phone buzzing and vibrating. Missed calls and texts from Rosa and Hope. I peeled the caked on sleep from the corners of my eyes, regaining my sight. Hope's text came first. "What happened? I have a place in Queens, call me"

Then Rosa's, "Everything ok? Going to church in morn with mom, and martha."

I sent each an identical reply, "Are you up?

Then I stumbled out of the bedroom and down the hallway, pounding on the doors as I passed by.

"Let's go boys, time to move out."

The coffee maker kicked on earlier than scheduled, rendering its energizing elixir available at the perfect time--now.

I received two almost identical replies from my earlier texts. One surprised me,, Yes, getting ready for church. I'll call you later." One didn't, "Yes, getting ready for church. I'll call you in 5 minutes."

"Let's go guys, we need to move out. You can sleep on the way to Queens."

"Queens, man. What's in Queens?"

"Your new home, now get your butts up."

My phone vibrated. "Hi Hope, good morning."

"I don't have much time to talk right now. Do you have a pen?"

I opened a couple of drawers, looking for the proverbial "junk" drawer every kitchen seems to have. Finding it on the third attempt, I rummaged through the junk, finding a pen that didn't work, and a pencil with no point.

"Can you text it to me?"

"No. I'll hold till you find one.'

I searched frantically with no success.

"Reef, where can one find a pen in this place?"

"On the counter by the microwave," he yelled back.

"Okay Hope, I got one. Go ahead."

She gave me the address of a vacant apartment one of her friends manages. We can use it until she leases it, or we put the plan in motion, whichever comes first.

***

Rosa's alarm pierced the quiet tranquility of her sleep, ruining her dream--right at the good part. Seven-thirty already, seems like I just went to bed. The sweet aroma of Earl Grey brewing in the kitchen forced her out of bed.

Rosa, Martha, and her mother stayed up all night talking about everything possible. With Martha present, Rosa expected the talk to somehow direct itself toward God. It did, but not in the way she anticipated.

She believed Martha used too strong of an approach with her God, which she discounted and resented. Last night though, it seemed tender, sincere, and real. She felt love radiating from Martha's heart--so real she could touch it. As the love magically found its way through the fortress she'd built over the years, she sensed a redeeming spirit come over her. Along with the love, she also encountered a vulnerability she couldn't describe.

Another surprise came when Rosa's mother admitted she'd experienced a similar conflict of love and vulnerability when she'd given her life to the Lord four months ago. Martha explained how the two emotions work together, forming the foundation of faith. She defined faith as putting your trust into someone or something that cannot be seen.

The therapeutic conversation last night helped her mental state, but she felt the physical strain all over her body. After downing a strong cup of tea, and spending a few minutes with her mom, she started the shower to get ready for the day.

Once dressed, she went back to the kitchen, where perfectly toasted whole grain bread along with another cup of tea awaited her. I love my mother!

Rosa heard the horn in her driveway. She peeked out and saw Martha's car out front.

"I'll be ready in two minutes," her mother yelled from the guest bedroom.

"Okay," Rosa responded as she walked out to Martha.

"Do you have time for tea?" she asked Martha. "Mom is almost ready."

Martha pointed toward the door. Mom stood there, "Do you have a Bible, Rosa?"

She walked toward the house, "No, mom, I don't."

"It's okay. We'll get you one after service."

★★★

Rosa kept a few paces behind Martha, and slowly made her way toward the main entrance. Various groups of people forming informal circles conversed. By the looks of it, they really enjoyed each other's company. A few shouts of "good morning" greeted her on the way in. Rosa acknowledged them with slight head movement, but tried not to make eye contact with anyone.

The line of people waiting to enter the sanctuary moved along casually. She followed mom to the back of the line, looking everywhere except right at someone. How long had it been since she last attended a Sunday service?

Three couples stood at the entrance, creating a passageway, the men standing across from their wives, she assumed. They welcomed each person before they entered the magnificent building. She felt anxiety as she approached.

While waiting in line, Rosa saw an old friend from the neighborhood. Her anxiety increased, but before she could turn around he said, "Rosa Milano?"

"Yes, John Walker?" she replied.

"Yes," he said, and gave her a hug, sending her anxiety into orbit.

"Teresa, this is an old friend of mine, Rosa Milano," he said.

"Hello Rosa, It's a pleasure to meet you," she said, giving Rosa a hug as well.

"Mrs. Milano?" he asked Rosa's mother.

"John Walker," she said. "Haven't seen you in years. We need to catch up sometime."

"Yes we do," he said. "How's your husband?"

"Doing much better, thanks. He's off on his quarterly golf weekend with his father and brother."

"Cool. This is my awesome wife, Teresa," he said as they exchanged hugs.

"Wow," he said. "It's great to see you guys. Enjoy the service. I'm sure you'll be blessed. We'll catch up afterwards."

They greeted the others, and headed toward the sanctuary. A nice seat in the back would be great.

Before she could get inside, she heard, "Rosa, there's Pastor Randy. Let me introduce you two," John yelled from outside.

Wonderful. So much for being incognito.

"Come on Rosa, he's a great guy."

John took off toward Pastor Randy while Rosa stood by her mom. John grabbed him and walked him over to them.

"Pastor Randy, this is some old friends of mine, Rosa Milano and her mother," John said.

"Betty Milano," Rosa's mom said, and shook his hand.

"Is this your first time here?" Pastor asked.

"Yes it is."

"Being this is your first time here, are you currently active with another church?"

"Yes," Rosa's mom said. "I live upstate. Just visiting for the weekend."

"And you?" he asked.

"No, actually I haven't seen the inside of a church in many years," she replied.

He nodded his head, "Maybe we can talk about it after service," Pastor said. "Right now though, I need to get going. Service is about to begin. It's a pleasure meeting both of you."

"Thanks," Rosa said.

As Pastor Randy walked off, Rosa told John and Teresa she'd catch up with them later. She wandered around the lobby, briefly making her way into the sanctuary. The back row had empty seats. She grabbed three of them.

She looked around in amazement. The place was packed. There had to be a thousand people or so here. The stage looked more like a concert set-up than a church service. A full band accompanied by a choir with at least 25 singers.

A young man walked up to center stage and said, "Welcome to the house of God!" bringing cheers and applause from the crowd. "Please take your seats; time to worship!"

Martha and Rosa's mom grabbed hands and started toward the front.

"I'm good back there," Rosa told them.

"Nonsense," she replied. "It's okay up front, I promise."

"Please," Rosa asked. "I'd feel much more comfortable right here."

They took the two seats next to her.

As the band began playing, people started clapping, and hands were lifted up all over the room. Rosa stood there mesmerized. This was nothing like church 30 years ago. After several songs, she joined in the celebration. She soon felt a weightless sensation similar to last night. What I saw amazed me. What I felt blew me away!

Several people walked on stage, praising God with a love and passion she had never witnessed before. It was difficult to understand what most of them said, but when a young lady stated, "God is in this house" everything changed. Rosa closed her eyes to pray. She lost touch with her surroundings, entering a place of divine love and hope.

Once the service ended, they made their way out of the sanctuary. John and Barbara stood by the door thanking people for coming. Rosa placed herself behind them waiting for the right opportunity to talk.

"Did you enjoy the service, Rosa?" Teresa asked.

"Enjoy does not come close to the right word," Rosa replied. "I think mesmerized fits better."

"I agree," she said. "Are you married, any kids? We have a great youth ministry here."

"Separated and expecting," Rosa replied. "But there's complications. I'm not sure we'll both make it through."

Rosa saw the tears develop in Teresa's eyes.

"Would it be okay to ask you why you say that?"

"Pre-eclampsia," Rosa answered. "Actually an untreatable strain of it."

She looked at Rosa as the tears flowed down her cheeks.

"I know it well, my dear," she said. "I experienced it with my first pregnancy. I miscarried early on."

"Not to compare, but mine is the really bad strain," Rosa said, "the one where we both can die during delivery. The only option I have is to terminate the pregnancy, which I could never do."

"Wow," She said, reaching out to pull Rosa close. "The Lord got me through it, and he'll get you through it as well. He's blessed us with two foster children, which we just adopted."

"I have heard people say many times that God works in mysterious ways. I'm beginning to understand how," Rosa said. "Thank you for sharing. Maybe we can have coffee and talk more?"

"I'd love it," Teresa replied, walking over to the information counter. She wrote her name and number on a card and handed it to Rosa. "Call me this week," she said. "I'll find time for you."

"I will, thanks." They embraced before Rosa left the church.

She had many unanswered questions in her head. One thing she knew for sure--God is real; and in the house.

Monday February 6, 2012 07:00 AM

Chief Moore woke in the best mood possible. The last year had its share of controversy for sure. Now it's time to put the finishing touches on "Operation Geronimo" and receive the accolades he so richly deserves. He's waited a lifetime for this moment. Who'd of thought an anonymous tip would bring it all together.

In three hours he'll make the arrests of Ty Gillian and Andre St. Pierre. Once they're in custody, it'll only be a formality to bring the charges against Green to the grand jury where he'd be assured of an indictment, allowing the case to proceed.

With Harvey dead, Stephens getting his immunity, and St. Pierre instantly deported, they'll be nobody left to tell the real truth behind the case.

Hawkins will get a nice promotion and bonus for putting this together. He may even get a shot at replacing Moore, once he's sitting in the Attorney General seat.

"Hawk, we still good for 10:00?"

He broke open the first of two jumbo eggs by cracking it on the edge of the iron skillet. Bacon, eggs, and pepper jack cheese is a breakfast he could eat every day. There's something magical about bacon. Add freshly ground coffee with creme brulee in his "I love Grandpa" mug, and the perfect meal is underway.

"Yes, all set. I'll pick u up at 0930."

While the eggs were simmering, he opened his email, and composed a new message.

"Bob, today is the day we make the arrests and put the case to bed. I'll call you once completed. Congrats on your successful campaign, 30 days to your next step."

After putting the breakfast and half a pot of coffee into his belly, he picked his favorite blazer from the closet--the same coat he wore during Green's arrest. How fitting to wear the same one when he brings the last criminal in this case to justice.

With nothing left to do at home, he holstered his weapon and headed to Queens.

***

"Lieutenant Rogers Please."

"Who may I ask is calling?"

"Agent Cody Hawkins, from the IPB. He's expecting my call."

"I'll put you right through," she said.

After a brief silence followed by a series of clicks, he answered.

"Lieutenant Rogers speaking."

"Hey Jim, Cody here. Are you ready? We'll be arriving on scene at 1000."

"We'll be ready to rock and roll. You give the signal and we'll handle it from there."

"Once Chief Moore confronts Gillian--just as we discussed."

"Got it." End call.

Hawkins put the phone back in its holster. Operation Geronimo will go down as one of the biggest busts of all-time. He mixed his pre-workout drink and set out on foot to the gym. Strenuous morning workouts prepare the mind and body for the massive stress days like today can generate. The other option, practiced by most of the agents, is heavy drinking, which creates a whole new set of problems. He learned to avoid this option early in his career.

After the workout, he headed back home to clean up and get ready for the occasion. The prescribed dress code for storming a house mandated wearing Kevlar body armor. It wouldn't be necessary today. No gunshots would be fired, but there'd be plenty of action.

His instructions for the day came directly from the top. Meet up with Moore at the prescribed point three miles away from the house, drive together in his car, and personally make the arrest once they confronted Gillian and St. Pierre.

He grabbed his weapon, his badge, and his sunglasses and headed to Queens.

***

Ty spent the entire night perched in a wing back chair looking out the third story window of their new, temporary home. I can't take this hiding anymore. It's time to stop running. Time to defend myself and gain back my freedom.

He walked into the living area and grabbed the pre-paid cell Reef provided.

Three rings later, "Reef," he said. "I gotta get out of here, man, I can't take it anymore."

"I met with Hope and Rich last night," Reef replied. "It'll be over soon, I promise. As a matter of fact we're heading that way now. Get your buddy up and both of you be ready when we get there."

"Where you taking us?"

"Just be ready," Reef said. "We'll explain when we get there."

"Okay, but I'm telling you, I can't take it anymore. And Dre's not doing any better. He's about to flip out."

"I got it," Reef replied. "Just hang tight for another couple of hours."

★★★

Hope met Reef at the cafe where she and Hawkins had coffee last week. The safe house sat less than half a mile away. They talked over the strategy and walked to the building. They entered through the basement and walked up the four flights of stairs. They stopped before entering the hallway and texted Ty to open the door.

The apartment entrance was directly across the hall from the stairwell door. Once Ty unlocked the door, Hope and Reef rushed in locking the door behind them. She felt the adrenaline flowing through her body initially making it hard for her to breathe.

"Hi guys," she said. "You ready to move again?"

"I'm ready to quit running," Ty said.

"Me too, man," Dre added.

"It'll all be over soon," Hope said.

"We need to do this in an orderly fashion," Reef started. "They know you're here, and will be coming for you in 15 minutes. So right now let's get moving down to the first floor. Follow Hope."

They grabbed their stuff and started out.

"Hold on," Hope said. "No need to take your stuff. We'll come for it later. Come on, I'll lead the way."

Ty went first, followed by Dre. Reef stayed in the room placing Ty's personal cell phone in the room. The GPS locater would confirm their position. He kept a safe distance behind them in case someone followed them.

Hope exited the stairwell first, and took a look in both directions. Seeing it clear, she ran across the hall to unlock the door. She stood inside the janitorial closet holding the door open. She poked her head out again, and seeing nobody, waved Ty across. She followed the same ritual waving Dre across, then closed the door with all three of them safely inside. After explaining the process, she slipped out leaving the door unlocked.

Reef waited for Hope in the lobby, facing the doors the police would be storming in less than 10 minutes from now.

★★★

Chief Moore waited impatiently for Hawkins to arrive. The anticipation of the upcoming arrests and celebration left him short of breath and shaking. His heart was pounding against his rib cage so fiercely he could almost hear it. After a couple of long, deep breaths, he felt his pulse slowing. Come on, Hawk. Where are you?

Within seconds he saw Hawkins pulling up behind him. The Chief checked his watch to confirming the time. Perfect. He grabbed his backpack and clipboard and waited outside his car.

"Right on time," he said to Hawkins as he entered the car. "Let's go make history."

Without a reply, Hawkins depressed the accelerator, leaving rubber tracks and burnt rubber fumes behind.

"You ready Hawk?" Moore asked, still shaking from the excitement filling his veins.

"Yes," he replied. "I texted Rogers before picking you up. Everything's a go."

After a series of turns, the building came into view. On any other day, Moore wouldn't even notice the dingy, aged building, or the low-life tenants occupying it. Today though, it symbolized success. Achievement he'd yearned for. Accolades well earned, though never granted. Today is my day.

Hawkins phone chirped, "Agent Hawkins," he answered. After a few seconds he hung up. "Showtime!"

He swung the cruiser up onto the sidewalk directly in front of the double glass entry doors swinging his door open before stopping. Moore followed suit. As they headed toward the door a uniformed cop stopped them.

"Wait here boys," he said. "We'll go get them."

"Out of the way, pal," Moore replied. "This is my bust. I'll take care of it."

The cop looked at Hawkins.

"Chief," Hawkins said. "Let them go in, we'll wait right here."

"Okay," he said. He walked backward away from the doors. Eight officers in full body armor rushed into the building. Two went up the stairwell; two into the elevator, two waited in the lobby, and the other two ran down the hall, presumably to another stairwell.

Moore leaned up against the front of Hawkins car resting his hand on his weapon. He noticed more uniformed officers fall in line behind Hawkin's car. Nobody's going to escape this.

What seemed like an eternity, in reality took less than three minutes before the lead officer escorted Ty Gillian and Andrew St. Pierre down the hallway toward the doors.

Moore stood up straight and put his game face on. As they exited the building he took three steps toward them. He prepared himself to speak the words, the magic words when all of sudden Hawkins came up from behind.

"Chief Moore," he stated. "Hands on your head. You're under arrest!"

"What the hell are you doing Hawkins," he screamed. "I'm supposed to be arresting them."

"Now," he repeated. "Hands on your head."

As Moore turned around to confront him, the same two heavily armored, well built, officers who took down Rich Green, pinned him to the ground stripping his gun from the holster.

"You heard the man," one of them said. "Hands on your head."

"You'll pay for this Hawkins," Moore screamed trying to work his way loose from the officers cuffing him. "You don't know who you're messing with."

"Take him away Lieutenant," Hawkins barked as he answered his phone.

"Awesome, great job," and hung up.

He promptly alerted his superior on the results.

"Sir, Hawkins here, Operation Geronimo completed. Moore and Stephens In custody."

Monday February 13, 2012 1:00 PM
Judge Carter's Chamber

Hope led us into Judge Carter's chambers. Attorney General Pines, Agent Cody Hawkins, District Attorney Baines, and the court reporter sat around the long conference table waiting on us.

I sat across from Pines, with Hope to my left, and Ty to my right.

"Gentlemen," I said nodding my head in respect.

"Strange turn of events over the last 72 hours," Pines started.

He looked across the table, taking a few seconds to stare at each of us.

"I'm shocked," he continued. "I mean, I knew Moore could get crazy, but never imagined he'd ever stoop to this level. Due to uncovering the set-up, all criminal charges will be dropped."

I smiled at Hope. Ty dropped his head and exhaled a heavy breath in relief.

"There's still, however, other issues we have to contend with," Pines said. "But first, how'd you know Moore was behind all of this?"

"Well, in retrospect it was easy to spot," Hope answered. "Stephens involvement, the uncanny coincidences behind the companies, and the new Chief," she said pointing to Cody Hawkins. "He confided in me about the internal investigation into Moore's tactics. He was actually on a sting, and when Moore selected him to work the Geronimo case. Well, the rest is history as they say."

"Good work, all of you," Pines stated. "Let's deal with the remaining issues."

"Such as?" Hope asked.

"Even though your clients have been victims of entrapment, the law clearly states all inside information must be disclosed, not acted upon. And, well, you guys took the information and profited on it."

I leaned back putting my hands behind my head, you're kidding right?

"How can any of that be admissible?" Hope asked. "It's all part of the entrapment process. You can't possibly be willing to continue suit against my clients using evidence from another illegal activity."

"Not criminal," Baines interjected. "Civil penalties must be assessed in this type of case. Agree with it or not, your clients used insider information to profit. That's illegal."

I looked at Hope, then Fines, while pinching the bridge of my nose with my thumb and index finger.

"What are you proposing?" Hope asked Baines.

"Well, we can sue for up to treble damages as per the law," Carter said. "We have a big time investor charged with four counts of illegal activity. Then the whole murder, entrapment thing. We have to show the public we stand for justice."

"Meaning?" Hope asked.

"We'll be working out some sort of penalty," Pines said. "It'll be significant and send the right message to our constituents. You broke the law, and you must pay the price. It'll take a while to compute the financial portion. The other side is owning up to the wrong-doings and accepting your ban from ever working in the financial industry again."

"May I speak?" I addressed the room. "I'll own up to everything I did right now. Ban me forever, I don't care. Take all my money, I still don't care. I want this nightmare to end so I can take care of more pressing matters in life. Where do I sign?"

"I'm with him," Ty added. "It's time to find a real job."

"We'll be in touch with the court date," Baines said. "Expect a sensationalized drama once you're in court."

"So we're free to go?" Ty asked.

"Yes, but don't leave the city without letting your attorney know," Baines replied. "And don't discuss the terms or this meeting with anyone not present in this room."

Ty got up from the table. "So I can just walk out of here?" he said pointing with both hands toward the door.

Carter nodded.

"Adios, Amigos," he said walking out the door.

Monday February 13, 2012 3:00 PM

I walked out of the courthouse ecstatic. Hope stayed behind to work her magic on Pines and Carter. She wanted to start the fine negotiation now, instead of waiting on the state. It could be an advantage for us to move quickly.

"Hey Baby,done call me"

I called Reef while I waited for Rosa to return my call. As usual he answered on the first ring.

"Rich, you're a free man I take it?"

"Yes sir," I replied. "Free from jail time, thank God. The civil charges are yet to be filed--they'll be substantial."

"I don't imagine you'll be in too bad shape afterward though."

"Are you kidding me? I still haven't seen your bill."

"Or Hope's," he added.

"Thanks for reminding me," I replied. "Which cars do you want?"

We both laughed.

"I'll also need a job, if you know anybody hiring a criminal."

"What about Ty? How'd he handle it?"

"Once Carter said we're free, he took off." I heard the incoming call clicks and looked at the phone. "I'll call you back, Rosa's on the other line."

"Hey baby," I said. "We just got out of Carter's chamber. All criminal charges are dropped, but we'll be facing civil penalties, and from the sound of it, they'll be substantial. The good news is no jail time."

"That's great," she said. "Hiring Hope paid off, didn't it?"

"Heck yeah! She stayed behind to start the process of reducing the fines. How's your day? How're you feeling?"

"Not real good," she replied. "Getting bad headaches, and feel sore all over. I threw up twice today."

"Oh, baby. Is there anything I can do?"

"Afraid not," she replied. "I'll just have to learn to deal with it."

"We'll have to learn how, Rosa. We're in this together, you and I, all the way."

"We need to make room for one more," she said.

I can't believe I left out the baby.

"God needs to be the foundation of our life and relationship going forward," she said. "There's no way either of us can handle what we're about to face without His grace and love."

Now I really feel dumb.

"We'll talk about it later, Rich. I need to get to my next patient. Love you."

"Love you too," I said. End call.

I found a spot on one of the benches outside the courthouse not covered with bird droppings, and sat down. God? Martha must have gotten to her.

Wednesday February 22, 2012 3:00 PM

I entered Green Gardens through the main gate. I drove past the monuments taking in the serene setting, making my way to the office. The leafless, large oak trees spread their arms, casting huge shadows over the plush over-seeded lawn resembling a professionally manicured golf course. The sculptured shrubbery clipped to perfection, leaving no branches out of place. The expansive collection of roses, now dormant, is still kept in immaculate condition. No sucker growth and no dead blossoms. Winter annuals and perennials put the finishing touch on one of the most beautiful places I've seen. Too bad Green Gardens is a cemetery.

I circled through the parking lot and headed back out to the grave sites. Row 35 to be exact. I grabbed the winter bouquet from the backseat rearranging each stem of every flower so they accented the tombstones perfectly.

Walking down the pathway, I recited out loud the name chiseled into each head stone. This annual event terminates in front of 35e and 35f. Here lies Mr. Harold Anthony Green and his beloved wife, Suzanne Celeste Green, my parents. I carefully placed the red flowers in front of my father's stone and the yellow ones at my mother's. If my prayers are answered, next year they'll still be two graves to visit--not four.

My appointment is with salesman/ curator Billy Thomas. I maintain a first right of refusal for the two spots bordering each side of my parents. Although I believe Rosa and the baby will make it through, I'm taking no chances. By the end of the day, Billy will have made his easiest sale ever. Plots g and h will belong to me.

Thursday, June 2, 2011 11:00 PM
Hospital Room

I've played and replayed this scenario in my mind hundreds of times now. Each and every time I come back to the same answer.

The only person who can make this decision is God-- and I'm not God.

I got down on my knees, closed my eyes while raising my hands to the sky.

"God, I've not spoken to you much in my life, but that doesn't mean I don't believe you exist. How can I possibly be expected to make such a monumental decision concerning two other lives? If it's about me, fine, I'll accept that responsibility, but not when it comes to my wife and unborn child."

The tears oozed from my eyes down the sides of my nose.

"Please God, put your hand over them. Whatever happens from this point on will be considered Your will. Let it be done."

My tears became larger, streaming down my cheeks onto the floor.

"Thank You Lord. Thank You for hearing my prayers tonight."

Rosa lay there fast asleep. Monitor leads glued to various places on her body make her look more like a science experiment than a beautiful woman about to go into labor. I wonder what she's thinking? Is she praying as well?

***

I waited by her side all night without sleeping. My adrenaline continued to flow. In less than one hour, my life will be altered forever. For all I know, this may be the last morning we share together. I'm going make it worthwhile.

A slight tap on the door bought me back to reality.

"Who is it," I whispered toward the door.

"Doctor Sorensen," she replied as she carefully pushed the heavy wooden door open entering the room.

"There's a few things we need to go over before she awakens," she said. "We can use the office down the hall if you wish."

"Right here is good," I replied. "There's no way I'm leaving her alone. Not even for a second."

She waved me over by the door where she stood.

"I know it's a difficult decision, but have you two determined the course you want to take?"

The anxiety of this decision has taken quite a bit out of me. I now realize, more than ever, the preciousness of life.

"We've decided to go ahead with the birth," I told her. Tears started to well up in my eyes once again. "God will determine the outcome. This is not for us to decide."

She looked at me and gently nodded. Her deep compassion rang through loud and clear.

"I'll do the best I can for you two." She tried to smile as she left the room. "Buzz me when you're ready."

"Thanks, Doc. I will."

Once she left I closed the door and sat down beside Rosa, grabbing her left hand in mine.

"Rosa, baby," I spoke softly. "Time to wake up my love."

Her eyes flickered, and she flashed her warm smile.

"Hi Rich, is it time?"

"Almost, baby. Almost." I gently brushed her hair away from her face, staring into her sparkling brown eyes. "Are you sure about this, Rosa?"

"Yes, Rich. I'm sure. I'd never be able to overcome the guilt and remorse if I didn't try." She looked away toward the window, then back straight at me. "I'm sure; call them to come get me."

I walked out of the room down the hall to the nurse's station. As I approached, they all stopped talking and focused on me.

"She's ready," I said. "Can we get started?"

"I'll call Doctor Sorensen," one of the nurses said. "We'll start the prep once we get the okay."

The next hour stretched the limits of my patience, my strength, and my faith further than I'd ever been stretched before. Doctors running around, tubes and needles poking in and out of Rosa's body, and machines beeping created a chaotic environment.

Once Sorensen entered, I had to leave. The complexity of the procedure prevented non-medical personnel from remaining in the operating room.

I hugged Rosa, "I love you Baby," I told her. "Everything will be all right, my love."

She pulled me close and kissed me on the cheek, then on my lips. "I know. God is in complete control." She winked, pointing to her belly, "We'll see you in an hour."

I walked to the waiting room in a daze. I grabbed the first chair and slumped down in it. A few seconds later I broke down, whimpering and crying like a baby in front of everyone. I felt a soft hand lightly touch my shoulder. I looked up. Martha stood there with a man I recognized as Pastor Randy of the church she and Rosa attend. Next to them stood Reef, Ty, Hope, and Stanley.

"Thanks for coming," I said nodding my head acknowledging their presence.

Pastor Randy stood in front of me while Martha rubbed my shoulders in an attempt to comfort me.

"Rich, may I ask you a question?" he asked, and sat down next to me.

I nodded.

"A serious question?"

I turned toward him nodding again.

"What is your desired outcome?" he asked.

"For both to survive--of course."

"What if one can't?"

"Then I leave it in God's hands. How can I decide who can live and who can die? A decision like this can't be made by man."

"Both of you've thought this through and agreed?"

"Yes, but I've accepted the fact only God can determine the outcome. All we can do is accept or deny it."

I looked at him and saw a nurse approaching from behind. "Mr. Green?" she asked.

"Yes."

"You can come back now," she said, and walked toward the delivery room.

We walked past the nursery on the way to the delivery room. I stopped at the large window watching the newborns fuss and cry. Life is such a precious gift. Will baby Rich be in one of those cribs in a few short moments? Only God knows the answer.

"Mister Green?" she called to me. "Are you ready? It's time."

Am I ready? I had my doubts.

Two Weeks Later

I woke up early, forcing myself to make my final trip to the cemetery. I pulled in front of the plots leaving the car running.

"Was this the answer to my prayers?" I shouted toward the sky.

"To be left alone. No wife, no kids, and no business. You're supposed to the God of mercy, grace, healing, and love. Where is it? Where's mercy? Where's grace? How about healing? How can I recover from this?"

I fell to my knees.

"What kind of God are you?" I screamed. "Talk to me! Don't destroy my life and just leave me hanging. I need answers."

I felt the pain swell up in my heart, finding it hard to breathe. I worked years to build an empire and it's gone. Just like that. I repented to save my wife and kids. And they are gone. Just like that.

"You told me to trust you Lord. What do I do now? Where do I go from here?"

I wept for what seemed hours when I felt a hand on my shoulder. Startled, I fell on my side. Reef bent down offering his right hand.

"Sorry, Richie, didn't mean to scare you," he said, lifting me up. "Lock your car and come with me."

I brushed myself off and wiped my eyes. Hesitantly, I joined Reef outside his car.

"Where we going, Reef?"

He pulled me close.

"You prayed for guidance and direction. I'm here to help you find it."

ABOUT THE AUTHOR

James Castellano was born in New York, joined the Air Force in 1979, and remained in Texas ever since, with the exception of an 8 year stint in beautiful Emmaus, PA.

He and Rosemary married in 2002, have 6 adult children, 2 grandkids, 2 dogs, and a Quaker parrot named Jones. After traveling throughout Texas, they settled in Waco, where they have a thriving Financial Advising business.

James and Rosemary are members of *The Church of the Open Door* in Bellmead, TX, and support several ministries in the area. Most notable, *The House Where Jesus Shines*, a full-time residence helping inmates successfully transition back into society.

A huge Oklahoma Sooner fan, they can be found in Norman, or in front of the TV every Saturday during football season. James is an avid golfer, sporting a handicap of 18.

James also wrote *E-Short* articles for the *Enrichment Journal* focusing on Christian based Leadership principles. These will at some point find their way into another book.

CPSIA information can be obtained at www.ICGtesting.com
Printed in the USA
LVOW03*1733040915

452519LV00005B/15/P

9 780996 428507